Vicki Viidikas was born to an Estonian father and an Australian mother on 25 September 1948 in Sydney, New South Wales. She was educated at various schools in Queensland and Sydney until the age of fifteen when she left school to work at a series of casual jobs, including a stint at Abbey's bookshop in Sydney. At age sixteen she began writing, and never stopped. Writing became her passion and her life. In 1967 'At East Balmain' was her first poem to be published. Four books which comprise both fiction and poetry followed: *Condition Red* (1973), *Wrappings* (1974), Knabel (1978) and *India Ink* (1984). All met with critical acclaim and over time Viidikas has become a much anthologised and influential writer. In 1975, Stephen Wallace directed a twenty-five minute film entitled *Break Up* from the short story 'Getting it all Together' published in *Wrappings*. Robyn Archer recorded Vicki's poem 'O Woman of the Moon' for her 1977 album *The Wild Girl in the Heart*. During her writing career Vicki travelled widely and lived in India, on and off, for more than a decade. Her interest in Indian life and culture and the Hindu religion was reflected in her writings, particularly *India Ink*: a collection of prose poems written in India (1984). She continued to write prolifically through the eighties and nineties up until her untimely death on the 27 November 1998.

*Works by Vicki Viidikas:*

# WRAPPINGS

## Vicki Viidikas

Introduced by Jane Grant

ETT IMPRINT
Exile Bay

ETT IMPRINT
PO Box R1906,
Royal Exchange
NSW 1225 Australia

Copyright © The Estate of Vicki Viidikas, 1998, 2022.

First published by Wild & Woolley in 1974.

First electronic edition published by ETT Imprint 2022.

ISBN 978-1-922698-47-6 (pbk)

ISBN 978-1-922698-48-3 (ebk)


Some of these stories originally appeared in *Tabloid Story*, Sydney; *Nation Review*, Melbourne; *Stand*, Newcastle upon Tyne, *Tharunka*, Sydney, *Westerly*, Perth; *Coast to Coast* - Angus & Robertson, Sydney, 1973; *The Outback Reader* - Outback Press, Melbourne, 1975.


Cover photograph by Geoff Goldberg.
Cover design by Tom Thompson.
Internal design by Hanna Gotlieb.

# Contents

# Introduction

*'It was at some very wild poetry reading rock n roll band happening night in a dance hall in Glebe. I sang back up with the band and danced my arse off. I'm a great dancer, and really was billed to read poems, and Nigel Roberts was there, and Bill Beard, NZ heavy weight hipsters and Kate Jennings or Jean Bedford, seething agro feminists, the Balmain Bohemians. I said I loved Bukowski, Genet, Samuel Beckett, William Wantling ( junkie poet), Sylvia Plath, Billie Holiday, Michael McClure – they so totally attacked me. Oh yes DH Lawrence, Ted Hughes- shit was I 'heavy duty', maybe mad, destined for the street … a nihilist, a ball buster, shit they went right over the top at my taste in literature, one of the fems slapped me so I hit her back hard. Bill Beard took me outside for a joint to 'calm down.'*

Vicki Viidikas 'How I lost my sense of humour (in Australia)' unpublished[1].

In 1976 when this, or something like it happened, Viidikas' second collection of 31 prose poems and stories had sold out of the hardback edition and had just been released in paperback, John Tranter calling it 'one of the most interesting books of the decade'[2]. *Wrappings* plays across categories of fiction, poetry and polemic, often shifting form within a single piece: 'This is not even a story' the persona states mid argument with a male writer in 'The Incomplete Portrait'(p.116), *Wrappings* part manifesto and part expression of a new Australian realism.

Vicki Viidikas was born in Sydney on 25 September 1948 to an Estonian violin maker and Australian mother, the parents separating from an unhappy marriage when she was three. Moving between NSW and Queensland with their mother and 'staying with relatives and in boarding houses' was 'disruptive and unsettled', older sister Ingrid Lisners recalled. Viidikas was their father's favourite. He kept in touch 'with occasional letters and presents and visiting us in Brisbane' seeing them more frequently after they returned to Sydney when Viidikas was 13, the young writer connecting with her European heritage.[3] At 15 Viidikas dropped out of school, moved to cosmopolitan Kings Cross and began 'reading a lot of French writing, symbolist poets and surrealism' she said later in interview: 'writing out my problems', bringing out 'what's in there rather than having a concept, which you are quite conscious of, which you put down.'[4]

The teenage Viidikas was working in an art bookshop and sleeping in a friend's bathtub when poet Robert Gray met her. The first writer Gray had ever known he was 'fascinated that the work came to her as copiously and as naturally as rain', as if craft played no part. A short-lived, although creatively supportive marriage to the painter Robert Finlayson when Viidikas turned 18 offered shelter, the couple moving across town to the bottom flat in 'Onkaparinga', a rundown waterfront mansion in Johnston Street Balmain, colloquially known as 'Cockroach Towers'. A plump faced portrait of Viidikas, painted by Finlayson for the Archibald Prize, shows how young she really was when her poem 'East Balmain' was accepted by *Poetry Australia* in 1968.

Poet Kerry Leves meeting Viidikas in 1968 noticed an 'already somewhat battered' Penguin edition of *A Rebour* by the French decadent novelist Joris-Karl Huysman, translated in English as *Against Nature* (or *Against the Grain*), on her bookshelves. "'Oh, you must read that!'" she said. Its importance to her lay in a 'kind of contrariness' Leves thought, 'going against the accepted ways of doing things', a model as much for the life as the work.[5] Her association with John Tranter and Robert Adamson's belated modernist revolution, overturning rigid poetic structures, begun that year in Balmain, was cemented a decade later with her inclusion in the *New Poetry* anthology edited by Tranter, alongside Adamson, Tranter, John Forbes, Martin Johnston and the only other female voice Jennifer Maiden. A first collection, *Condition Red*, was published by University of Queensland Press in 1973, followed the next year by the Wild and Woolley edition of *Wrappings*, the fiction showing the same 'contrariness' as the poetry.

Later, much would be made of Viidikas' unconscious

processes, automatic writing, the furious pace she wrote at without revision, drawn from her readings of the surrealists, a view of the work that Viidikas led in an interview with *Australian Literary Studies* in 1977. *Wrappings* also shows conscious, crafted literary correspondences. 'Viidikas urged on us Baudelaire' Leves recalled of workshops they attended in the late 1960s[6], the French symbolist's exhortation in *Fleu du Mal* 'in repugnant things we find charms', which she first read as a teenager, was an aesthetic Viidikas continued to model in *Wrappings*. Rattling off another long list of the writers 'out of step' with society who had shaped the work to *Australian Literary Studies*, Viidikas cited the gutter realism of Bukowski as imprinted on her studies of prostitutes, pimps, drug dealers and strippers in *Wrappings*.[7] In dialogue with dead and living writers, *Wrappings* ends with a challenge to her peers: 'The page should fuck back. I can't think of a more reasonable premise.'

The stories in *Wrappings* are about stripping back the delusions, romance, lies, mythologies and cliches the personas and portraits hide behind. 'Wired Out' addresses psychological truisms, and is probably an example of 'the problems' the teenage Viidikas was working out on the page. Originally called 'Wrappings', the story was first published in the University of NSW student magazine *Tharunka* in 1970, although its setting in a boarding house 'closet room', somewhere like Darlinghurst in the days before group houses, and her habit of sketching experiences at the time, suggests that the story was written earlier. 'Wired Out' deals with a teenage girl's sexual grooming by a real sugar daddy, feeding romantic fantasies with marshmallows and Darrell Lea chocolates, the final encounter between girl and man deflating expectations of trauma: 'moving away from the closet, a new job, once she met him up the Cross and he was living with someone from Les Girls and she'd met a man, and he just laughed patting her bottom.' (p.55).

'The Silk Trousers' and 'Voulez Vous?' draw on Viidikas'

first trip to India, the UK and Europe in 1973, funded by a Commonwealth Writers Grant, the tourist bringing back a broken roof slate from 'Wuthering Heights' and her ticket from a Miles Davis concert in London. Dropping out is an ongoing theme. The lesbian drifter in 'Steve and the Big Smoke' references a character Viidikas met at the women's separatist commune Amazon Acres in Northern NSW, where the writer stayed on and off in the early 1970s. More typically allusions to the Back to Land movement are sceptical: The self-centred hippy in 'It's Just the Full Moon' cutting loose in the city; or boredom in 'Love an Apple', playing out around the sound of a man typing and the smoking of the last joint, hope fading that friends from the city will visit with more drugs.

'Cooling off', set in hospital ('your petal face broken off'), is one the most disturbing of the confessional prose poems, written shortly before *Wrappings* was first published in 1974. Viidikas was travelling in a campervan with her boyfriend when the primus stove she was lighting exploded, setting her on fire. She put out the flames by jumping out of the van and rolling on the ground, her sister recalled.[8] Viidikas was in hospital for many months, Robert Gray seeing her 'with her Nordic hair cropped and her eyebrows gone, and her face peeling, although it would end up unmarked.'[9] The writers rallied. Geoffrey Serle, head of the Literature Board, put together a fund of six hundred dollars towards 'medical expenses,' as he explained in a letter to Viidikas dated April 1974. Treatment took up most of that year. In November the Australian Society of Authors organised a benefit for the quaintly phrased 'poetess', as advertised in *Education,* the journal of the NSW Teacher's Federation, with readings by David Malouf, Robert and Cheryl Adamson, and Nigel Roberts, the audience advised to bring their own blankets and flagons of wine.[10]

Cocaine, marijuana and heroin wind through the stories, sitting Viidikas uneasily in the company of Nigel Roberts, Robert Adamson and Michael Wilding, the Balmain writers and poets who wrote about taking drugs. The 'hipster' poets and 'suave dudes' Viidikas called them in her unpublished fragment, who never danced. The first publisher of *Wrappings* saw commonalties, releasing it the same year as Zimmer's Essay, Robert Adamson's collection of drug poems and autobiographical short novel on his time in prison and becoming a poet, co-written with counterculture *The Digger* journalist Bruce Hanford. Zimmer's Essay tracks the romantic line of the poet/outlaw/seer back to Arthur Rimbaud. Viidikas didn't sit herself in this lineage. She wasn't interested in the 'literature of myth' as she calls it in *Wrappings*. (p. 116); thought Rimbaud's cult status, together with that of the American Beat writers Ginsberg and Kerouac, 'overblown.'[11] Drugs in *Wrappings* are defences. They keep reality at a distance in the sadomasochistic relationship between pimp and girl in 'Stuffing', or in the weekend lost to cocaine in 'The Snowman in the Dutch masterpiece.'

How 'taste in literature' could erupt into a feminist brawl in 1976 becomes harder to see with time. Viidikas was vague, couldn't remember who exactly she 'hit hard', but it might have been Kate Jennings, whose seminal 1975 woman's poetry anthology *Mother I'm Rooted* includes a poem by Viidikas. Jennings was also a poet. Her first 1975 collection *Come to Me my Melancholy Baby* was 'seething', culminating in the proto rap 'Moratorium: Front Lawn 1970', eviscerating the male demonstrators as misogynists and their passive girlfriends as complicit in their own oppression. Poetry was political for Jennings. She and Viidikas didn't connect. Viidikas was sitting the confessional mode of Adrienne Rich and Diane de Prima in the masculine cityscapes of Baudelaire, Genet, Burroughs and Bukowski, her problems technical rather than ideological. 'Vicki's work is partly about showing that a woman can do it too' Leves thought later, writing it 'from a female perspective, out of her life.'[12]

Viidikas might have disliked 'sloganeering', as the inside flap to the Wild and Woolley hardback edition tells us, the work striving for a realism that avoids ideological conclusions, but the publisher's packaging of stories that 'never proclaim sisterhood or liberation' is curious:

*'You don't want to read about me in a VD clinic waiting to have my*

*vagina scraped' the persona says to a male writer in 'The Incomplete Portrait': yet
'you'll read Burroughs's description of gouging holes in his thigh to try and find a
vein. You'll read that and say there's some point to it — he's a junkie who may
influence others not to take drugs, having some positive effect on society -
because his experience is so vividly ugly. Yet a woman writing of an
instrument stuck up her cunt is 'being self-indulgent', as the doctors make
notes. And you won't read of the girl who was gang raped, preferring to
refer to statistics and 'she probably asked for didn't she'. You will think
these stories unnecessary, indicative of a female mind gone sour* (p.118).

'The Incomplete Portrait' channels the same philosophical
reclaiming of the female 'infected, resurrected body' as the radical
edge of the women's movement Viidikas ran into at the Glebe rock
'n'roll/poetry happening. The persona's position on
femin-ism, however, is unstable. DH Lawrence, another
one of Viidikas' suspect heroes, is deployed in further
provocative argument. The word was out Kate Millett
thought Lawrence a 'fascist and a womanhater' the
persona says. 'Maybe he didn't succeed, but wasn't he railing
against sexual strictures for both men and women?' (p.119).

Other contemporary female writers who knew
Viidikas thought her ambivalence to feminism more local and self-
protective. 'They set themselves up as the gatekeepers' poet
Anna Couani recalled of the mainly male Balmain literary scene.
'Vicki saw them as her peer group and wouldn't separate from them,
was worried that if she adopted a feminist type of attitude, she'd
be alienated from them.'[13] Viidikas did feel trapped. 'I was never
charming' she wrote in her diary: 'intense and angry yes. Intellectually
aggressive but there it ended. Why bother to talk when the
feedback was so bad? Talk tough and reject sexism and the
guys reject the female talker. Oh shit. I thought my fellow
artists would be wiser than all this.'

Most mainstream critics hated *Wrappings*. Hal
Colebatch, reading her as a new breed of feminist social realist
writer, demurred that 'we would be quite prepared to read about
scraping her vagina if it had a purpose … if her characters
'Weltanschauungs could be bigger - if they could be allowed to

at least display evidence of some awareness of the abstract notions of loyalty, deep love, human dignity, or something.'[14] Colebatch and Viidikas' Burroughs reading writer had a lot in common. They both thought stories about passive female bodies being acted upon viciously or casually by pimps, cocaine dealers, hippies, doctors and writers 'unnecessary'; her 'camera,' as Colebatch called it, not art. He was right though about the social realism of the fiction – stripped of politics and propaganda – capturing 'the realities of subcultures' as she told *Australian Literary Studies* in 1977, in work that prefigures dirty realism. The transgressive new photography was actually a very good analogy. Viidikas' confronting portraits are very like the photographs her contemporary Carol Jerrems took of Sharpie culture in Melbourne.

The stories in *Wrappings* written 'out of life' were new in 1974 and difficult to place. Australian fiction at the time was always looking backwards on an imaginary past, forgetting that white foundation writer Henry Lawson was sketching his contemporary world. Balmain short story writers and editors Frank Moorhouse and Michael Wilding were important exceptions and influences, their monthly publication *Tabloid Story* driving a new contemporary fiction, its clever design as an inset magazine to alternative and mainstream newspapers ensuring wide reach. Viidikas was an early contributor to the first 1972 edition, along with the stories by Wilding and Moorhouse that fictionalised each other and were set in Balmain, their middle-class Bohemia as remote from Viidikas as Thomas Keneally. *Wrappings* peels back all 'literature of myth' including Balmain:

*All these bits, these bits. He's written a story about it, that X was lesbian and Y came over to shoot up Mandrax in the bathroom. He wasn't there but his girlfriend rang him to say, come over and get me out of this. I don't know what's happening. Lock yourself in the kitchen. It's your scene he said, then went back to sleep. He wrote the story the next day.* ('Reality Fragments' p. 93.)

We might also wonder who the model for Roberto was in 'Christmas and the Detonator', although to chase the biographical sources would be to miss Viidikas' point. After drinking all the booze, smoking other people's stash, and complaining about the smallness of the Christmas chicken, Roberto is last seen: 'huddled in the corner readings aloud from Flowers of Evil, jittering as DTs come upon him (been an alcoholic for ten years). 'I just love these poems' he intones, as his left leg breaks into a spasm across the floor.' (p. 101). Roberto reads Baudelaire, but Viidikas doesn't tell us whether he is a poet. Roberto unwrapped is simply an oaf.

Helen Garner was a rare critic who saw the art in *Wrappings*. Then a journalist and feminist working for the alternative newspaper *The Digger*, and on the verge of turning her diary into *Monkey Grip*, Garner puzzled over the verisimilitude of the work:

*Maybe it's a bit simple of me to imagine that the girl-persona's experiences are those of, or based on those of Viidikas herself. But they're so extraordinarily convincing, real and familiar that they must be. The people, the situations and dialogue are so familiar that some of the stories might be letters you'd written yourself, or conversations you'd overheard in some restaurant.*[15]

Viidikas never wrote about the domestic. Her newly liberated woman in the story 'Getting it all Together' creeping out of a man's bed before dawn 'so Tony wouldn't wake up in the morning and wonder who we were' (p.37) is much more cynical than Nora in *Monkey Grip*. Nonetheless there are obvious parallels between the inner-city group houses, the casual sex and drug taking and the confessional female personas, always reading and listening to current music. More significantly, Viidikas shows Garner how to 'write out of life' the transcriptions of real conversations/real people Garner spots in the work, which gives *Wrappings* the authenticity that the counterculture so admired. Garner's blend of the real and fiction is seeded in her early reading of *Wrappings*. It is only by seeing *Monkey Grip* is in dialogue with *Wrappings*, moreover, that Viidikas as vital missing link between Carlton and Balmain can be understood.

The challenge was answered more problematically by Viidikas' publisher and former lover, Michael Wilding with *The Short Story Embassy* in 1975. Dedicated to 'Vicki', Wilding's comic novel is about the beautiful and enigmatic young poet Valda held captive by two fiction writers (based on himself and Moorhouse) in an old Balmain mansion, a little like 'Cockroach Towers', and forced to write short stories. Wilding, an academic in the English department at the University of Sydney, was possibly making a critical point: Viidikas was a better fiction writer than poet. Further wilder, demonic representations followed, turning her from 'oracle' to 'witch' Viidikas noted dryly in her diary. The characters troubled Kerry Leves, but when he 'tried to quiz her about "Valda", Vicki shrugged - writing was (is) an open field.'[16] He thought it damaging, as he told Jennifer Maiden. 'The issue is not with the representation of an actual fictional persona outside the writer's self' Maiden wrote recently, 'but with the writer's insecure need to internalise it, continue to be imprisoned by it and continue to project it.'[17]

Wilding sent Viidikas a copy of *The Short Story Embassy*, although she never replied. Of course, abstract beliefs that writing is an 'open field' and what it feels like to read a version of yourself don't necessarily align, whether Viidikas or Wilding internalised representations of themselves or not. Viidikas had laid down a literary challenge and, as in *Wrappings*, for all its self-exposure, damage was best kept at ironic distance: 'These wrappings are extremely interesting said the psychiatrist, poking at a pool of tears. ('Wrapping: Part Dialogue' p.66).

In 1976 Viidikas thought she'd 'drown in cynicism and the bleeding hearts club' if she didn't get out of Australia. Awarded another Arts Council Grant to write a novel, 'a rock n roll bible' about 'a babe looking for the Holy Grail. Herself, still',[18] Viidikas planned to write it in India. She'd already moved out of Balmain, although its influence was more difficult to shake: 'When I finally learn to grow up I'll stop going on about the agonies of men losing their erections, flunking out in bed, or intellectual gymnastics turned nasty' she wrote in her unpublished fragment. 'No I'll get my sense of humour back in India and write out Wilding and Moorhouse.'

JANE GRANT

# Notes

1. All unpublished writing including diary entries and letters cited are held in the Vicki Viidikas Collection, Australian Defence Force Academy, Canberra.

2. John Tranter, 'Growing old gracefully: the generation of '68', *Meanjin*, 37 (Apr 1978); republished in *The Temperament of the Generations: fifty years of writing in Meanjin*, edited by Jennie Less, Philip Mead and Gerald Murnane, Melbourne University Press, 1990, p. 271.

3. Ingrid Listners correspondence with Tom Thompson, 27 July, 2022.

4. *Australian Literary Studies*, vol.8, no.2 (October 1977), p.155.

5. Robert Gray, *The Land I Came Through Last*, Giramondo, Sydney, 2008, p.303.

6. Kerry Leves, Foreword, *Vicki Viidikas: New and Rediscovered*, Transit Lounge, Yarraville, 2010, p.17.

7. Kerry Leves, 'Constructing the poetic past: A response to Jamie Grant', *Southerly*, 60, 1( January 2000), p. 157.

8. Ingrid Lisners, 27 July 2022.

9. Robert Gray, *The Land I Came Through Last*, Giramondo, Sydney, 2008, p.304.

10.     *Education*, vol. 55, 19 (November 20 1974), p.381.

11.     Gray, 2008, p. 304.

12.     Leves, 2010, p. 21.

13.     Pers.com., 22 July, 2022.

14.     Hal Colebatch, review of *Wrappings*, *Westerly* (December 1974), p. 74.

15.     Helen Garner, 'Books for fascination', The Digger, issue no.37 (October 30, 1974), p.10.

16.     Leves, 2010, p.16.

17.     Jennifer Maiden, *The Cuckold and the Vampires: an essay on some aspects of conservative manipulation of art and literature, including experimental and the conservatives' creation of conflict*, Quemar Press, Penrith, 2020, p.32.

18.     Frank Moorhouse (editor), *Days of Wine and Rage*, Penguin, Ringwood, 1980, p. 417.

# Trying to Catch the Voice

I'm not quite sure when it was, the first time I wanted to say something about myself, that I was quite definite I had to speak, and someone would listen. Whenever it was it was early, I wanted to run into the darkness and start talking to the night, standing in that black tent, a voice in dark veils, imagining an answer. Or walking about in daylight addressing myself to the sunshine, calling out as it drew me out, to be turned like a mute thing, to be cooked and gone brown. Maybe it was the trees I imagined had ears, putting my arms around their knobbly trunks, laying my face against their skin as they stood there tall messengers.

So much time has claimed the chase, talking to stones or flat eyes of pools, paths worn into mountains, miles of thin sand, waves hushing and knocking. Things have been loved and fallen, lies burnt to death, and still I want to speak, still words die and new ones come, been talking and writing words down, read words aloud and seen them poised bright daggers above people's heads.

Scratching words in sand and seeing the waves absorb them, being anonymous yet waiting for answers! hiding behind words and exhibiting myself in front of them - none of this has been enough. Finally words remain to be written as though I've never heard them before. Finally I cannot have done with them, a voice persists though it offers no goal, no complete and absolute meaning.

# The Snowman in the Dutch Masterpiece

She stepped into the blue Jaguar, a piece of sky fell away almost as blue, as he closed the door swiftly behind her. They sped silently across the Harbour Bridge, lines of traffic poured multi-coloured streams into a waterfall of light which fell away to nothing. 'The menu is very good,' he said, flicking on a cassette of Hendrix; two speakers in the back of the car pushed out perfect sound, perfect reception.

A million lights gleamed lavishly as Julia leant her arm on the window sill. She smoked a perfectly rolled joint as Hendrix wailed and fell through 'Foxy Lady,' 'Hey Joe what'cha tryin' to do?' Buses, legs and hats floated past the window. She was going outwards, going away from the city and this perfect stranger was driving.

At the top of the restaurant stairs he guided her to a shadowy corner, brass lanterns threw an orange glow over their faces. Delicious indefinable smells drifted by, waving. She felt anonymous under her shiny cap of hair, beautiful, it could have been anywhere.

'Oysters to start, then coq au vin, etc. etc.' The order could have been flaming yak's tooth, stuffed tortoises or sixteen Kiwi rissoles - she was being handled expertly, and he was smiling.

Dinner was superb and through it he talked of Bangkok, Afghanistan, Nepal, opium houses in Calcutta. 'They have tiled floors with hard mosaic headrests for pillows and a cistern of tea bubbling out the back. An old man sat with me to keep the pipe burning okay, and I just smoked and smoked, you have to lie down, and go into a dream baby, you just dream your day away. Sometimes I'd get a rickshaw back. to the hotel and read a book or maybe play some dice or sleep. It's beautiful baby, it's a good life, a good trip.'

They lingered over coffee and she knew then he'd take her to his apartment. 'I've got some very fine dope there, I'll drive you back in the morning.'

Well he wasn't so handsome, he was sharp with dark eyes and his face sunken a little in just the right and enticing places. Faded jeans, sterling silver belt and black leather jacket, $200 on his back and a Moroccan leather wallet. He was distant and unbuyable, could afford anything that night. He had Chinese ivory cards, a ritual where the chosen mustn't move too close, even at the risk of coldness, rigidity, of not having anything to lose.

Steering her to his car he said his apartment was temporary till his current deal came off, then he'd fly again to London. 'The place is cool, that's why I chose the North side. It pays to appear like everyone else.' Obviously. 'I could be any other businessman, a young designer on the make or any well-heeled executive.'

The car flowed in through a pair of high white gates to a lawn with potted palms, blood-red rose bushes, a private beach with water lapping at the end of a slender pier. Safety devices, spy hole, the door so white in the darkness she felt she was entering a gilded cage, a shrouded and unwalked kingdom.

Not even the black leather lounge could unnerve her, its round openings like glistening fleshy stomachs. Not even the Thai silk lampshades, an enormous stereo, the television with its tinted blue screen, the perfumed toilet paper. She laughed at the perfectness of it and, 'What's amusing?' he asked, but she was thinking of flea-ridden terraces, peeling walls, junk-filled back-yards, friends opening cans of soup. The rusted typewriter, sordid poems. They called that freedom, the price of wanting to know who you are. And here she was being treated like a decorative object, nice sometimes, like buying candy, something special. But think of poems in soup cans.

'Sit down babe, I've got some very fine whisky,' appearing with a decanter, ice cubes, glasses, ashtrays. 'I've just come into some very good cocaine, do you dig coke? you do? fine,' he materialized a silver box from Bali and took out a bag and tiny ornate mirror. Tipping a small white heap on the mirror he handed it to her. Like that.

Maybe $40 worth. She licked a little with one finger then sniffed slowly. As her tongue, nose and throat went numb he smiled taking off his jacket, the belt flashed on his hips.

The whisky was so cold it ran down her throat like a hard steel stream, a glittering avenue in her body, she could feel her face melting. A record was playing softly as they nodded and dreamed in the arms of the black sofa.


'You have a very fine figure babe, ever put it into movies? You can get very good bread in Hong Kong for blue movies, you know, nothing too off, that's up to you, just have your boobs and cunt photographed, that sort of thing.'

'No,' she said, 'No I haven't,' trying to tell him how she'd chickened out on a job in a disco for the very reason she didn't like flaunting her body, leading them on knowing they'd remain empty-handed. 'Prick teasing,' she said, 'You know if they so much as lay one finger on you there's ten bouncers to throw them out. It's crazy! getting paid for giving them nothing,' and she felt she sounded so moral, so lame... 'Peep shows.'

'But they dig it babe.'

'Yeah but I guess it depends on how much you want the bread eh?' 'But babe, what are you going to do without bread? You can't make it without it. I mean, give the suckers what they want, why worry about what they're getting? They aren't going to feed you for having ideals. Sure I can dig what you're saying, those jobs are pretty degrading really, I guess it's different for a chick, but why be missing out on comforts because of their ignorance? They're only crass pigs.

'I tell you, what do you think I'm doing? A few more hauls and I'll be sitting sweet, I'll be able to say fuck off to all those gigs, let them rot in their nine-to-five lives, their peephole nights out, I ain't going to pay for their stupidity! Hell they don't even know how to have a fuck! If I'm prepared to take the risk of going in the can for ten years and put up with their moralizing shit: You're selling your soul, You're corrupting our society, to make some loot to get away from them, then hell babe it's better, I'll be free to have ideals ... I mean I'll have the bread to do it then, won't I?'

And she sat back silently feeling like a two bob watch slowly ticking the hard way. He leant over and touched her face. His hand felt cool and strangely unattached to anything, something distant out of snow, glossed over depths. 'Another whisky?' he filled her glass.

Standing by a huge bay window she looked out over the beach where yachts were moored just off the shore, like giant pale insects their bodies frozen, wings flickering gently. It was unreal, a reality so super real it was unbreakable, timeless. Everything fitted as perfectly as a Dutch masterpiece, the milk frozen in mid-air, the picture so pure, the girl's face a white mask.

He seemed to be asleep on the other side of the room, so she took her drink and a transistor into the bedroom and turned on the lamp. Soft yellow light seeped across an immaculately made bed. Turning back quilted satin covers she undressed, arms and legs pouring from the clothes, long hair streaming down her back, red feathers, red and white and yellow into the sheets.

It could have been hours later she felt him next to her, long arms around her waist, his face on her breasts, licking. He murmured and kissed her throat. It was snow everywhere falling and melting coolly inside and outside her, ruffling the feathers, red and yellow, he was a running snowman, dark and brown, hard and soft . . . distant. He didn't seem to like her touching him, pushing her hands away, he turned and placed her just how he wanted, remaining separate, in control.

But she wanted to erupt, wanted her skin crawling breaking the images of pale cool masks, plaster hands, lips: she wanted to drink the milk, break the glass, carve up the painting, this masterpiece of perfection, get out of the frame. But the snow remained, drifting them out to sea.

'Snowman snowman you'll get through ... ' that song ...

His ritual was complete. 'Want some hot chocolate?' disappearing in a silk dressing gown to the kitchen, returning with cups, cigarettes, 'It's good coke, isn't it,' and she nodded, dazed, unable to feel happiness, everything fitted in the cage.

Noon sunlight flooded into the room as they woke to the radio still playing. He said he'd had a fine sleep, 'fine' was always his word, everything was fine, fitting. 'You've got fine skin babe,' eyeing her with a critical expression in the daylight. And he got up and went to make breakfast, came back with a tray, percolated coffee, eggs, etc. two tightly rolled joints. 'I always like to have a smoke in the mornings, makes you relax into the day better I think.' Perfect. Perfect. Clearing away the tray, 'I'm sorry I don't have much for you to read,' tossing down a few *Time* magazines. 'I know you dig reading, I haven't any poetry, I'm not into reading much myself.'

So she lay around flicking through magazines, eating halva, smoking and painting her eyelids blue while he made a few mysterious phone calls in another room.

Mid afternoon he announced something had come up and he wasn't going to the city till late that night. She had nothing else planned so they drank some whisky and sat around playing records. He amused himself reading a travel book on the Far East, kept asking her if she was comfortable and apologizing for not having any 'literature' for her to read.

While he was away buying some more dry for the whisky she curiously went through his drawers. Silk shirts, a snake-skin belt, gold bracelets, a diamond watch. He had very few possessions, one each of a few essentials. There were no books, trinkets, phone numbers, photos, no papers to show his identity, that he voted in Bengal or had a property in Texas, a wife or communist grandmother. It was weird. He had three suitcases and a mink coat because he dug, 'soft things against my skin.'

'It's a damn shame a chick like you doesn't make something out of your looks.' They were sitting on the lounge drinking whisky with the Stones.

'What's this writing jag going to do for you anyway, there's "no bread in it, and those shits won't recognize you, assuming you've got something to say, till you're ninety-nine and dead in a crummy room by your typewriter, cockroaches crawling over your slippers. Then they'll lay a claim on your stuff, call it "another great work of art" and make a lot of stash out of it. And I bet you'll say you don't want to write shit books for bread, so what's it going to do for you, keep your soul pure?' and he snorted into his drink. 'I think you deserve better than that babe. Why shouldn't you?' And hell it was really nice grass they'd been smoking and she couldn't think too straight, Julia was feeling nothing like Julia, and it seemed those things he was saying were kind of making sense, kind of getting to her. She couldn't very well define that 'pure soul' he'd scoffed at.

'I guess I just have to do it,' she offered.

'Perhaps it's a matter of life styles.' Poverty? Madness?

'I don't care about money.' Not true! She'd had dreams about bacon, huge strips of it walking towards her juicy and friendly - being able to afford bacon with eggs for breakfast.

'It makes me feel real, I know who I am then.' Rubbish! The million faces leering back at her. All her own.

'It seems natural,' dubiously, 'It's not a question of money or lack of it. It's trying to understand things, see things, you know, make something.'

'It's like quality, the quality of things, people, food.' Andersons bacon. Home on a pig's back. Ghastly generalizations. 'Yes!' she sucked at her drink like a fish at air. 'No, it's not that simple,' drifting off again.

'Ah honey, you're crazy! You don't have to do anything to prove yourself to those shits.' (Which shits exactly?) 'They're blind anyway. They won't satisfy you. Come here beautiful,' he pulled her close to him, playing with her breast, almost bit the nipple off. 'What about some more coke eh? Relax.'

Out came the little mirror and they swallowed some with water this time. The leather lounge squeaked and rustled as she felt all that snow descending, softening words, meanings, smoothing things out; the day was any day, any time.

The Stones rang through 'Satisfaction'. 'Paint it Black', 'Let it Bleed.' They oozed along the lounge together, Julia, the snowman, snowing in that room, under their skin, coming closer together, apart, distant though their bodies touched, catching sight of each other, falling, not knowing who the other was, forgetting, strange.

It must have been night, the phone rang and they both jumped like firemen. She could see him through a bright haze mumbling into the phone, then he wrote something down and rang off. 'It's okay babe, I don't have to go into the city tonight. So I can take you back anytime you want.'

'Oh thanks,' was all she could muster. Then, 'I'm feeling really good, actually I'm feeling brilliant,' getting up and wandering round the room. He smiled, 'Fine.'

Neither of them felt like eating so Julia decided to take a bath. She put in bath salts and sandalwood oil and brought in the radio and a heater. 'Want to take a bath with me?' she called. But he seemed rather annoyed, becalmed. 'No babe, I prefer to bathe alone,' so she undressed feeling self-conscious that she'd asked. Funny. As if there were rules and she was moving in too close.

'Tralalala trala trala,' she sang and chuckled in the bath, splashed, soaped her breasts and blew on them, listened to the radio, ran in more hot water, generally made a racket, she was feeling so good. He stuck his head in the door, 'It's only a bath babe,' then he was gone. She threw some suds at the back of the door. Funny. She was of course breaking up the Dutch painting, the milk maid was pouring milk all over the floor, lifting her skirts, dancing nude in the kitchen. Dropping her mask. Out of the frame.

They made love under the quilted covers again and she bit his shoulder and he said, 'Ouch,' and told her to stop it, and pushed her hands away. Silently. Controlling that intimate ballet. He told her to lie still and did she have to root around so much like a beaver, and she was mad and funny, and they were high and fine. Later he made them hot chocolate.

Next morning he brought in the breakfast tray with two joints, then drove away in his sky-blue Jag. 'Don't answer the phone, and don't answer the door,' was all he'd said, 'I'll be back in a couple of hours.' So she wandered round the flat looking at magazines, turned the TV on then off. There was just nothing in that gilded cage to involve her. No rubbish or disorder. It was perfection. So she mentally filled it with garbage.

Looking out through the blinds the sun was shining on the pier, the little beach was deserted. Boats were dead white, clean, moving ever so slightly, no one on board. Thinking of the Flying Dutchman, if she stared hard enough perhaps he'd appear on deck, the sails of his yacht be moved by invisible hands, unseen winds.

But there was no one. And he didn't want her to leave the flat, didn't want anyone to see her, even know she was there. So she undressed and got back into bed, listened to the transistor, drew pictures with an eyebrow pencil on the back of a *Time*, tried to write a poem. But she felt anonymous, frozen, like a beautiful vase in a glass case. Back in the frame.

She must have fallen asleep because he was bending over her, 'Hello doll, I've got something for you,' throwing a package on the bed. Inside was a novel by Colette and some short stories by Somerset Maugham. He grinned almost sheepishly, 'I hope they're all right, that's all they had in the newsagents,' and she said, 'Gee thanks, how amazing.'

They had coffee and a joint and he'd bought steak to cook for dinner. No one mentioned when she was leaving. 'Don't you think we could go for a walk on the beach, it looks lovely out there,' just on dusk, she was feeling restless. But, 'No babe, it's not cool really. I don't want anyone to know you're here. It's better for both of us,' he waved an arm towards a block of apartments near by, 'Never know who's in there, it pays to be discreet, even paranoid sometimes.'

He cooked steaks served with mushrooms, broad beans, baked potatoes, red wine. He told her he'd lived with a chick once who'd had a kid. And he'd packed her off with a few thousand dollars to make sure she and the kid would be okay. 'That's a rather big thing to do isn't it, giving her all that money?' Julia asked.

'Well I reckon it's the only thing I could have done, till she got a job and organzied herself. She was a good babe but I needed to be free, you know, if a deal suddenly comes up and I have to fly immediately, what do I do about her and the kid? She might not even want to go to Pakistan or somewhere, and she didn't.

Chicks always want something you can't give them. They just don't dig the fact you might want something other than them and a nice little domestic scene.'

'Yeah I guess that's true, but women seem to need the illusion that something is total, that there's something to completely consume them, anyway something other than the fragments ...' Julia was feeling very strange, stoned again and faceless. 'What do you mean, fragments? A chick can do what she wants, just as much as a guy. But they don't, that's all! They do some piddling thing and expect everyone to notice, to praise them eternally. A guy just takes a trip, smashes his car, makes some loot, gets a fuck - he just does it! That's how things are! Fragments!' he snorted.

It was very dark outside and they were alone with the remnants of a meal. Julia didn't know what to say any more, and he seemed to be feeling the same. Turning on the TV he flopped in front of it smoking a cigar. The screen lit up cars, stallions, stretch bras, cigarettes with extra length, jeans, flyspray, She stared at the piece of fat on her plate. She seemed a long way removed from her lopsided terrace with its rancid backyard.

There were a ton of words she called 'art' lying in a front room there. Along with cockroaches, rejection slips, four letter words dotted out, losses. Complaints. That was poetry? Art? She had exactly $3.65 in her purse and ten cents in the bank. No job. A house full of people referred to as 'friends' who read books, smoked dope, patched each others' jeans, etc.

She knew she needed money, food, a regular income. Why didn't she bash someone over the head and steal his wallet? Settle down as a secretary? Marry a rich old bastard? 'Keeping your soul pure?' that's what he'd said. So what about the buyers who really needed that fix, their eyes hanging out, just to stay alive? Too bad eh? You take what you need. Uh huh. The sum total was confusion.

He spent the night watching television while Julia prowled around with her eyelids painted brown this time. Staring through the blinds at the never-changing harbour, the perfectly empty beach.

Finally flopping into bed to read the Maugham stories. He came in later, deftly made love to her, followed by hot chocolate - eternally the perfect host.

Let me in, she dreamed, hammering on the door of a sealed room, a distant order.

In the morning over breakfast he announced he'd take her to the city that day. 'Take a shower, get yourself cleaned up, I'll drive you in about one.' She felt suddenly deflated and he'd gone off into another room.

On the way back the car glided like a porpoise through streams of traffic. They didn't talk much, he seemed preoccupied, aloof, just the Stones grinding and bumping out of the cassette. 'I'm going away soon babe, probably next week. I might see you when I'm back. I won't have time before I go. It's been fine,' touching her on the face, smiling into the Oriental future, the door suddenly closed, shut, the beautiful car melting away silently into the city.

Outside the frame, looking down at the dirty street, the twentieth century greeted her, offering its greasy mask.

## Love an Apple

The grass lay flat along the hill, under the wind, the silence thickening along the ridge by the sea. With every chance of nothing more than the trees rooting and uprooting and growing and dying, plants breaking out in new leaves, splintering and curling back into the earth, the constant, the constant hush and lull.

Inside the house the first thing to move was the cat flowing on four legs down a hallway to the kitchen, leaning this way in a floating cloud of fur and stripes, and that way with its fluid spine and sharply defined ears and eyes. The people weren't awake yet and the cat was looking for food; it moved surely without having to recognise or acknowledge the silence which was always there.

The first sounds of morning and footsteps drifted down the hall, the first-lit flame of the day boiling water for tea. The cat miaowed and rubbed against the woman's legs as she got out teacups and bread, mumbling to herself, still half asleep, getting a saucer and pouring milk into it. The cat drank its milk religiously then wandered outside to sleep in the long grass. The sun wasn't out yet and the sky was a dull silver above the sea giving off the noise of its own colour.

The woman sat on the back steps drinking a cup of tea, looking out at the trees and hills, hearing the ocean turning over itself just down the cliff. The same. The trees and landscape revolving their natural order. Every day. Nothing could stop the growth of the gums or ferns, not even bushfires or floods; nothing could stop the cutting away of the hills by the sea. Eventually. Everything died and grew again. The same forces appearing though each leaf was new and unique.

Every wrinkle was itself. Nothing more. No, it was no longer a question of nothing more. The day still touched her hair and nightie. The birds would possibly not always sing, but still did.

'It's going to be an incredible day,' the man appeared in the doorway, already dressed and drinking a cup of tea. The woman nodded. He reached for her hand, touching it in silence, then disappeared inside the house.

*I dance with silence*
*And the plumes of love*
*Are black*
*Black with the motion*
*Of purple and thunder*
*The shining*
*Skin of a mole*
*The joy of a rat*
*In dead night under moonlight*

Those hills in Wales that Dylan Thomas wrote of, that strange purple brooding out of his words, as if to understand their meaning you had to fully see their colour; to let yourself be bruised, gently. The hills. A dress. Someone's hand. A cup. The animation of every thing. A word. A poem. A shape. The pulse of the thing.

### *The entrances*

They'd moved out of the city twelve months ago, after households of chaos as if bombs had been dropped, ashtrays trodden into carpets, faces breaking into tears and joints, the trippers of love tripping and screaming, the pubs that would never run dry, the multiple busts and infidelities.

'Man I've had 200 trips, smoked $5000 worth of dope, drunk uncountable gallons of piss, fucked 300 women apart from my wife - we have this cool arrangement. Yeah live hard, die hard, that's the only thing to do.'

Can you take it, can you take the freak-outs and rejection, the incurable paranoia? How many times can you blow your mind?

'We all know that marriage is crap, working is crap, having possessions is crap; we're all artists and deserve to be free. Action, action, trips and thrills. We don't want to be old and end up rotting in an invalids' home; to have to support kids and a wife and work for the rest of our lives.'

Emotional blackmail, legal blackmail, peace-love-and-gentleness blackmail, the latest guru blackmail.

- 'Can't get no satisfaction' -

Old days and past hangings. Old friends been in the nut house, had abortions, been bashed up by the pigs, tried to commit suicide, been up north, had marriage - 'even tried that one', got unhooked, hooked, jailed, interrogated, defiled.

With so many friends dead, she no longer kept photos. The long scars on her wrist. Postcards of Hades. Friends still on the wheel of parties, scenes, 'where it's all at,' the perpetual 'keep moving' syndrome.

When they'd decided to move away, a friend had taken her aside quite seriously and said, 'But what are you going to DO out there? You'll turn into middle class drones if you're not careful. You won't be close to films or rock concerts, you won't know what's happening. I mean, if you were going to live with a whole bunch of others, well that'd make sense. But alone! Just the two of you! You're copping out in a way, you'll probably get sick of each other anyway. It's not enough. What are you going to do, talk to the flowers?

### Tramp Tramp Tramp

What had been done. A history of pain and what the Jefferson Airplane sang: 'It's taken so long to come through.' The private inside of chaos and madness, the kerosine and lit match image of existence, offered on a knife to tantalise. Die hard, die hard - that old cliche - a million dyings every day. Who are you, without identity? You can be a head, a straight, a guru, a bourgeoise, a housewife, a junkie, a lush, a square, a drag. What do you want that money can't bring you, or a god can't listen to? That sense of security knowing you're one of five million others in this town, who eat breakfast every day, have a job, a car, a house and probably a wife and kids.

### Who are you?

The woman got up and went inside the house. Music was spilling out from another room; the man was engrossed in writing words on sheets of paper. A record spun round.

She listened to the music in the back of her mind as she washed up and tidied things about the house. Perhaps someone would come and visit them. They hadn't had any visitors for over three weeks now, it'd be nice, perhaps they could have a smoke, she thought she still had a bit of grass left. She decided to go look for it, among vases of flowers, ferns, books and records, mirrors, shoes, cases and tins of paint. She found it in the music box, enough for a few joints, so she rolled one. She went to the man and asked him if he wanted to smoke it with her but, 'No honey,' he didn't.

So she smoked it alone, looking out at the silver sky and bent over trees. The chair she was sitting in grew warm as a pot of skin, and the books on the shelf with the 'great works of art' in them chuckled. She pulled one out on Bonnard and suddenly was drenched with colour, every painting swam in its flesh of brightness, every apple and orange was soft, yes soft, nothing was screaming. It was outrageous that these things could be so beautiful.

She wanted to run around and show someone, shouting through the trees, that someone might lift his eyes for a moment from the sweating machinery, the shoe-filled pavements, and love an apple, or a chair, or a hand. That simple.

### *That there wasn't easily anyone else there*

She was alone with the pleasure, just the house and her man in another room, and the music still turning.

Outside, the hills rolled of their own accord, without bridges or constructions. And the wind lifted a thin branch on a tree just outside the window, and tore off a leaf. It danced for a moment then fell to the ground. She watched it - having taken so long to come through.

## *Letter to Mr. Boo Boo*

Mr. Boo Boo there is sadness and people stepping soft melons in the ground, and tripping seed pips, them catching in their socks and being carried and dropped elsewhere - in rivers, under logs, in trams, they cannot be destroyed, only their shapes changed, their possibilities rearranged....

It's possible to keep on, many shadows pass and remain, many dark shafts keep functioning, the moments remain there, Under the currents there are seeds, just as under apples' peelings there is the core, complete with sections, elements four. O play this seeding, under trees, under sky, O play this seeding.

Mr. Boo Boo there is seeding, a vast sky which opens and closes, an indelible well of shafts and tears, a series of growths which come from darkness, a memory of roots and a heave into earth. There are seeds embedded in song, there is energy, space and time, and these needs, these needs, these needs ...

# Off the Boards

'Oh listen, my name's Julia, could you lend us a ten cent bit for the meter? I just want to cook a few eggs.'

'Sure.' They were standing on the landing leading into the tiny kitchen, and as Sandra handed over the coin she noticed how pale the woman's face was, no make-up, over-ripe, fat, like something gone off and drying up.

A gas jet blasted on and Sandra edged into the kitchen deciding to make some coffee. Her room was just walls, even the kitchen seemed better. Julia was dropping a couple of eggs into a saucepan. May as well talk to her, sit down, light a cigarette, sit there between the stove and bare walls, greasy sink and cold taps.

'I just moved in last night, some guy helped me - he had a car. You should have seen him carrying all my bags! God, the costumes I've got! All getting crushed!'

'What do you do?' Sandra flicked ash on the floor.

'Oh, I'm up the Cross, I strip at the Phoenix, that sort of thing, I'm a dancer you know. Are you from the Cross too?

'Yes.' Sandra rolled the cigarette around in her mouth, she'd only moved away to try and straighten her head out; always got so out of control in the Cross ... so it seemed. This place was near to it but far enough away to be out of the morass - not the same degree of things getting stolen, being busted . . . chaos . . . etc. All those hard edges.

'I reckon this place is okay, lived here long? At least it's close enough - I got sick of all these guys coming round to see me. I need a bit of quiet, you know, the club likes you to try and keep your personal life private from the customers. If you can. But some of them are so gorgeous,' she laughed like a big jelly heartily.

'Oh,' said Sandra, 'it's a bit of a dump really,' noticing how big her boobs were, hanging, 'but yeah, the Cross can get a bit much.'

'I've got a beautiful body,' Julia said, breaking open the boiled eggs, adding a ton of salt. 'That's why I strip, I like to show what I've got. I mean, well, when you've got a good body like mine, you may as well make use of it, that's what I think. And I always wanted to give something, you know, entertain people like. I could never learn to type ...

'You must wait till you see my strings! I bet you've never seen a dancer's gear before. No, well I've got a divine tangerine G trimmed with lime lace. I wear red pasties with that one, and my flaming peach wig. And the black! I must show youl I do a slow number with that, lots of grinds before I take the coat off. I wear a long black wig, set it myself, and red satin gloves and shoes. It really sends them wild. They like me to leave that onetill the last show, it sends them out itching!'

She smiled at Sandra then asked her for a cigarette. 'What's your name love, anyway?'

After Julia had eaten her eggs Sandra trailed along to her room. It was loaded with bags, paste pearls, tarnished gold earrings, scuffed satin shoes, brass tassels, torn fishnet stockings. 'Ever seen pasties? I've got millions.' She produced plastic bags: iridescent purple, candy pink, acid green winking and burning, tossing them around, they scattered among nylon harem pyjamas, day-glo coloured nighties, red bras, 'Never on Sunday' panties. Pasties dripping from boobs like they were running with milk. Thousands of blazing sequins, lights, screeching with colour, look at me, look at me. Sandra felt as if her eyes and head had been stuffed with sticky lollies, crammed with sugars, assaulted with excess ... she reached for a cigarette. No one else.

Julia took off her slacks and stood there in midnight blue panties, a fat white belly lolling over the elastic like a bloated eye. 'I got extra last week, this guy was so wrapped, we had cocktails and ended up on beer. He's got a cream Porsche, fast hands,' laughing taking off her blouse, spinning in transparent panties and bra.

'I'll do some numbers for you one day. Do you work? Huh well, one night. I'll do my green and then the black I was telling you about. I love dancing.'

Sandra leaned back in the sea of nylon, synthetic scales, the bed lit up like a neon sign. Puffing. Staring.

'Don't you think I've got a beautiful body?'

'Oh sure,' Sandra swallowed, looking at the white flesh, the rolls, the boobs hung precariously in the bra.

'I've always been told I had a good body, that's why I went into dancing. I couldn't be an artist's model, I like to move around too much,' and she pronounced the word 'arteeist' like she was proud of it.

'Ooh, my French perfume!' she shrieked, 'Luigi gave it to me when we broke up but I lost the stopper and a lot of it leaked out, but I've still got some.' She rammed a scratched bottle into Sandra's hand. 'Look, have some, not everyone has French perfume, you look like you need some.' Sandra rubbed some on her wrists. Poo. 'Thanks.'

She dreamed that night of Julia at twenty stone dancing in a washtub suspended in Paddy's market, her jelly legs beating, breasts swirling pendulums, arms outstretched beckoning to fish and chip shop owners, pinball playing bikies, stripping to pasties that disintegrated as they twirled, fraying elastic strings.

'What's it like to have no breasts? It must be crazy,' leaning over to bludge another smoke.

Not again, Sandra winced, she was always going on about it. 'Oh I guess I don'tknow, if I've never had them,' trying to be FUNNY.

'You're nice, you're so little. You know, it must sound crazy but I think of you like a daughter, kid sister or something. You look like you need looking after, I don't know, somehow...' Julia flounced into a chair and stared at her, all of one week's acquaintance.

'I mean, you haven't got a body like mine, something big going for you ... working in that shop ... a lot of guys like ... have any men?'

Sandra felt herself tense, 'Yeah I'm pretty small I guess, I never thought of it like that. Sure I have guys... sometimes.' But how to explain they weren't... weren't gentle? Available? Faithful? Like... they were supposed to be. Like a dry fuck in the back seat wasn't what it... Like a bottle of brandy to loosen her up... Like did she need a 42 inch set of boobs?

It didn't make sense reading 'literature' about couples meeting in the printed word, giving each other roses, cooking meals in bed-sitters, sharing showers and toothbrushes and holidays, cosy fuckings, hashish at an 'in' disco.

I wear an Isadora scarf, drive with Bill into the country (in a racy red sports), drink wine in a candlelit tavern, make love on a windy beach, standing on a hill with flowers in my hair, he says, you're the most beautiful girl in the world, I'll never forget your face.

I am wistful and strange and he adores the way I laugh.

I am fascinating and enigmatic.

I am fashionable and smart, a swinging hippie chickee, a clever fashion reporter, groovy photographer, beauty consultant and fabulous cook.

I am beautiful and look like a model; I am never hysterical or covered in spots.

I have a swinging life and 'where the action is;' I never have time to be lonely.

After a day of rewarding work in a trendy exciting city I loll in a luxurious apartment, smoking heavily with sunken cheekbones. I decide to wear my see-through crochet jumpsuit with patent platform shoes. I wear bracelets with hearts around them, Mary Quant face glisteners. Dave is superb company and will arrive at eight in his Volvo. He'll bring flowers and chocolates and money and love ...

Julia's room sparkled and glittered with mirrors, bars of tinsel, paste, half-eaten lipsticks, dug-out mascara boxes, caked make-up tubes. Talk, Sandra was thinking, don't just sit there, be her kid sister, fill up the silence, get her to grind for you, make someone laugh, for god's sake make an EFFORT.

'Have you always stripped? Is there enough work?'

'Yeah honey,' Julia chortled, There's always one kind of work - know dozens of people - the right kinds mind you, more like having a good time. And when you've got a beautiful body like mine, well ... you know, they all tell me I've got class, they know I expect them to treat me right.

'I want to study arts, you know, go to university. I've been told I'm brainy. They don't take just anybody you know,' strutting towards a mirror. I know. 'You've got to sit for exams first. When I think of all those gas fellas with their MGs, they know how to treat a lady. I like a man to be studying something. I used to go with a student, he was studying medicine, got into abortions and stuff. He was real brainy.

'I've stripped at a few of their parties, they thought I was great ...'

There must be something, if I met someone on a bus, an etymologist, a kind lunatic ... I want ....

Sunday. Julia had washed her hair and was fixing it in front of the bathroom mirror; Sandra threw down another book, stinking refined sensibilities, romance, and decided to take a shower.

'Oh hi, don't bother about me, you just take your shower doll, I won't even notice,' grinding something on to her face.

Sandra decided to put off taking her shower. Something else to do.

She sat on the edge of the bath and lit a cigarette, Julia automatically reached for one, who could refuse. With her red stretch slacks and Fabu-lace underwear Julia was fixing to go up the Cross and 'crack it'.

'I'm going to make it good, Sundays can be such a drag,' or something like that, shouting through her pancake make-up. She wore it like her face had been dipped in it, a line ending at her chin.

'You know, I think I might be pregnant, I feel like there's a baby in there,' banging her stomach, 'Christ knows whose it is, I don't care, you can still crack it up to eight months - did you know that?'

She applied some more eyeliner till you could hardly see the eyeballs among the darkness; Sandra just sat there.

'What doll, no fella tonight? Jeez you have a dull time kid, I ain't seen a fella with you since I've been here. What do you do? You shouldn't be so serious,' who was hunching on the bath positively green with embarrassment.

I need a velvet ribbon to tie up the empty dark. I need a brush to dust off my desires built on fantasies and cobwebs. I want a patch to stitch up the bitterness. At least she's got someone. Maybe that'll be me one day going off to 'crack it,' mooning over an Italian bouncer, batting false eyelashes pinched from Coles, pinching fat in a swollen mirror. Oh Julia, you're positively beautiful. So huge and warm. How many fingers squeeze those nipples? Who will want you when you're slack from use? Thinking everybody loves you. Painted doll. Tick. Tick.

I could've counted to ten and cut off all my fingers so I wouldn't have to touch anymore ... about what I wasn't touching. I could've stuffed myself on pastries till I was twelve stone and beds wouldn't hold me. Grown eight inches taller, discovered breasts and nylon panties, imitation jewellery and headless faces. This is insanity, you've gone off the boards, plunged off the last whitewashed plank. There is loneliness and need.

'See you later babe, if I score some bread I'll buy you a book 'cause I know you like reading.' Smiling, Julia sailed off down the stairs.

# Six

### Going

Sharp, clear images cutting up the sky. On a clear day you can see what is flat, blue, three dimensional or merely an illusion.

She stood at the station watching her cases being wheeled away; received her tickets from a man behind a sign saying *The Man in Grey*, and he was in grey. Incredible. She laughed, finding a seat by a window that didn't open, that was a wall between faces, moustaches, lips, hands on bags, in pockets, touching and weeping, fumbles with coats, tubes in shoes.

Blurred train shapes - she remembered flaked leather seats, bad coffee in paper mugs, clanking toilets that let out on to rails, farting under seats, faces reading or sleeping, hand straps swinging in empty corridors.

'No, I've never been here before ...' she leaned away from the man in the seat opposite, a boxer or something with a huge bungled nose, 'I'm quite okay thanks,' as the train pulled in next morning.

More legs and hands, another state, breaths sighing past windows, (will he still be glad I've come?) faces bursting like flowers into bloom to receive someone. She moved through the maze collecting her cases, into a cab, past pockholed clocks, wrinkled paper bags, hellos, lips plastic peeling off, lips in pockets, eyes rolled in collars, memories in bags, goodbye...

### Back

'You came here to shit on me, didn't you, (but I love you) I can't stand it. I love you I hate you, no, I don't mean that. (what do I mean) You can't leave, we can work it out, we can try again, (what) I'm going mad. Why are you going? (what's he got that I haven't) It can't be true, I'm going crazy. Why are we like this? (now I hate you).

Books twisted across the floor, throwing more, his hands slipped off the pages, words meaning lemon skins, desperate. And she crumbled and fell about the room, accepting his anger, not sure what she felt or what was the point, through clothes, vases, torn prints, half packed boxes.

'Don't go, but please, I don't want you like this. (I want you any way). Do you have to go, we can work things out. You're going? (who is he anyway) but I need you, (I love you) don't go.'

A burst of red flares off an isolated island, somewhere cut off, that needs all the connections but denies -

### Photos

'I'm going, we're only hurting each other by staying together. And this...' She threw her arms away, 'I'll write if you like, and you answer, will you answer?' (ever answer, no questions, this is no question or answer).

She piled some more books into a case (what to take, who could know what to take) with shoes and beads, clothes and a few stones. The place seemed no longer connected to her, she couldn't conceive of ever having lived in it. The connection was broken, new phones had been installed. The wires were there but no longer rang through.

And she could feel the pressure of many brightly coloured phones, ear pieces breathing, mouth pieces talking in strange distorted voices, crossed wires electrifying and buzzing with so much anger and chaos, word confusion. 'Do you feel the phones?' But he snorted, 'What are you talking about?' Ah. No phones. Messages. Button B bringing back damaged coins.

Next day watching her cases wheel away down the platform, she no longer felt phones, only spaces, as if all roots, sound boxes, nerves and connections had been ripped out, the ground covered over, and a remaining vacancy.

### Just Words

I can no longer remember your face. I can feel it there shaped in my head, in air, but nothing presses on the sides, there are no distinct features.

To remember a face on the surface of a well, a flat shape with no perspective, something that can be removed, peeled off like a sheet. A connected fur ball, thought ball, lining movements and skins; fur balls in drawers ... trying to keep things intact ... fur remembering ... no ... memories are fur.

Some weeks seeing Greeks with square haircuts in fleck jackets, bursting everywhere over arms, ripping in the streets. Then this ... She makes love (who is it) watching skies fold up into tents. She sees words clutter the streets, soles of feet march up trees, she finds stones in bathtubs. Letters arrive in the mail from a familiar hand. She answers in a familiar hand; the letters become unfamiliar ...

And goodbye, photos are meaningless.

### Moving

Night in the new city was like damp cloth. 600 miles away. Sitting on grass the ground came rushing up under her knees. She thought she heard beating. Something spread.

'It's so beautiful.' Wind made his hair move, and she felt she needed ... He got up and climbed a tree, feeling rough bark on his hands and neck, stayed there on a branch like a parrot with bark feathers cackling into the dark.

She left him alone and started collecting sticks, perhaps a dozen that'd fallen from trees. Building up speed she ran a few yards, threw the sticks into the air, heard them thud and rattle onto the ground. She stood still then walked towards them. They'd fallen in a circle and some of them had broken, forming more, yet the numbers were irrelevant. Under the crescent eye, bulbous moon face she saw a map of branches, covering of symbols, there, reading them with the back of her eye.

Somewhere he came down out of the tree, having no more need for it now he was tree. He looked at the map then took her arm, slowly leading her away.

### Action

'This is, and this is, I'd like you to meet ... ' In a pub the light is yellow as piss on wallpaper, thin soakings through, watery eyes, lips, everybody's mouth is bubbling, grog words, liquid veneers. Wet hands around glasses, drinking or chucking in the toilet from too much, too ... watching it swirl in the bowl and disappear croakingly.

At ten the ship rolls away, walls sag, everyone out, the tiles slosh over, there are shoe soles in the dark.

He pulled her on top of him across a car, its slippery wet grooves. And laughing, her mind like blotting paper, she couldn't remember ... she had no conception ... there was no reality ... she was trying to place ... only the body knew where it was.

# Getting It All Together

It had been raining on and off for two months, large wreaths of silver water falling from a sagging sky. Days would change abruptly from thick mouldy sunlight to leaden rain, early streetlights and damp rooms. It was hardly the sort of weather to feel secure, stable or anything else in. The skies opened and hair swelled into wet spaghetti, ink on newspapers ran and people constantly coughed and snorted inside volumes of overcoats.

It was beginning to become a drag. Wasn't it a time when people were supposed to be 'getting it all together'? and the rain could either dampen it or freeze it without mercy.

I felt worse off than most, living in a room where the weather notice-ably affected what could be done in it. When the sun was shining I'd iron all my clothes, maybe hang them up, take long elegant showers, finally get around to cutting my toenails, read Lewis Carroll, drink cheap flasks of brandy having fantasies of highballs, yachts, Spain and so on.

But when it was raining I'd sit there rummaging with papers, dirty clippings, a saucepan under the leak, turn to people like Beckett or good old junk Burroughs, pick blackheads out of my nose, discover my teeth were rotting, things like that, telling myself, look what you've ballsed up so far, your life's just a disgusting mess, all these dramas and frantic ... where's it all getting you? what do you think you're achieving?

I'd stride around furiously thinking, these tragedies are ridiculous, ridiculous! rush to friends' houses in gumboots and sou'wester shouting, that's the last affair I have with a Chinese, a Greek, a bikie, an Australian, a married man. It's only my emotional life that screws me up! I'm going to take it easy from now on, stay at home, play cards, subscribe to magazines, write overdue letters, live a quiet life.

God the rain washes out some dreadful things from behind cupboards, seeping through the woodwork.

And I'd sit there thinking about John of course, being rational, saying, things are going to be so much better now we've broken up, it was the right thing for both of us. I'm free of all those scenes, it'll be better next time, I'll never fall in love again. It's so good being alone, having no responsibilities, not worrying about keeping. him awake, treading on their territory or cooking meals the way they don't like. Now I can be completely selfish, dye my hair red if I want, and not worry about upsetting him ... them ... I'm a free agent.

The bloody rain, and I'd sit there thinking like this, the free agent squinting and conning myself into everything's going to be okay, yes okay, I'm a single lady again, able to go out with Lebanese in greasy black Fairlanes ... hmn ... but wasn't I going to bake cakes and read introspective novels and build something for myself that wouldn't get easily washed away next time? Next time? Snort.

But meanwhile I called it the sane life, the getting it all together controlled life. Control, I said, erecting it in six foot high letters flashing in my head.

But what's so bloody sane anyway about stumbling around in a dressing gown (done up with a safety pin as you've lost the cord, it's so long since you've worn one), trying to fry eggs and flop down peering over the top of your burnt toast at the man from the room next door who's stumbling around with cornflakes, which you loathe, and who formally says good morning, and you think who the hell is that, and do I have to answer, and what the fuck's so great about this?

The sane life? the stability and got it altogether life? You tell yourself it's okay, I'm cooling off, I'm re-adjusting to simple, more ordinary things, normal things, not extreme things. I'm not fighting and screaming and pulling my heart around. I'm giving it a rest, a holiday eh? I'm going to be in control from now on, no nasty fraying edges, everything's going to run smoothly.

And you run the word 'smoothly' over in your mind like a piece of sickly caramel. Ugh.

You wonder about the man from the room next door and if he's getting himself together too. And you sometimes hear his radio soft at night through the wall, as you lie in the single bed thinking, this is the life, it's so peaceful yet the more you see of him flopping in his run-down slippers you know he's just going about his normal stable life as he always does, sanely, a flabby man of thirty-five.

He's not to know your life isn't usually like this. I fantasise about him as we pass in the hallway with dog-eared toothbrushes and grubby plastic soap containers. Even in the bath I imagine ripping his gown off yelling, this is what life's about! poking at his rubbery flesh, biting off his ear lobes. It's the hair in his ears that aggravates me as we face each other over breakfast, silent, wretched, giant gulfs and crumbs between us.

So I realise I have no intention of getting off with him, he's so busy being normal he'd probably die of heart palpitations soon after. I plan a good screw in my course of 'getting over it' as I watch his hairy ears munching above his cornflakes.

Whatever happens, it's all part of the plan to get sane and healthy-minded and not remain hung up over John. Don't people always say the best things after a marriage or a bust up is a brief affair? Anyway, I don't want to entertain Lebanese in big sweaty cars right now.

The rain still plunges from the sky and I have a terrible time battling down Pringle Street with an umbrella and a box of groceries. One must eat, I say positively, as the wind howls around my ankles and I remember John and I always used to drive to do shopping.

Just after my umbrella gets blown inside out and sails off like a broken tulip, a car pulls up and offers to drive me home. Clutching my wet hair and trying to feel adventurous I get in, but he's fat, Greek, a house painter covered in specks who leers good naturedly at me. We drive home in broken English silence and getting out I thank him profusely, wishing he were someone else.

Whatever it's about, this sane life is getting me down. Friends are sympathetic in cosy terrace houses with husbands and regular lovers, fridges crammed with food, plastic bags fat with grass. I don't even have a joint back in my room, but they understand my situation having been in it themselves sometime in '65, '71, or six months ago.

They assure me we're all going through it - this reappraising one's life. Whatever happens they say, you're better off without John. I have to admit it was no good between us, and surely they coax, I don't want anything as bad as that again?

Babies, streets with no destination, faces, clocks that go off at the same time every morriing, empty coffee c ups, l aundromats, p eople s eem t o be giving birth, moving to the country, going to parties, or sitting back turning on and watching television, happy sloths. Couples burrow inwards making dramatic plans for the future. Others start drinking Fenugreek tea to rid their skin of impurities. There's talk of pollution and anti-noise committees. Two of my friends become vegetarians and attack me when I buy a hamburger. Everyone's talking about aggression and what we can do about it, we who have survived. I seem to have the term 'making it' constantly on my mind or other people's.

Oh world with your thousand stages.


Ruby and I venture out on a greasy Saturday night determined to get some action (she also being a free agent). The thick city air beats us in the face - cars, fish and chips, dirty shoes fill our nostrils. The streets are full of drunks, perverts, lavatories and teeny boppers. I wonder what John is doing now, if he could see me what would he think I was after.

It seems years since I've been out on a Saturday night like this, with another woman, and I tell Ruby it's like we're two tarts on the make. She laughs and says, didn't John and I just fight on Saturday nights anyway?

One way or another, after drinks, bus rides, leers, hoots and grunts from shadowy Chevrolets, we arrived at a party. The place was packed with people lushed or stoned, girls in platform shoes, with red cupid mouths and vicious fingernails; guys in sweatshirts, peace signs, studded belts and cuban heels.

We drank, smoked, burning our lips on roaches, having circular conversations. Hours later in a slum at Redfern I kept telling myself, this is the life, this is what you're after, keep you sane. Chuckling. Better than living with some possessive madman, spending Saturday nights at home fighting, trying to make it, weekends so predictable.

Ruby was laughing somewhere in another room and joints were being passed. Through a cracked pane of glass I saw a crescent moon riding the sky's dark face. Picking my way through empty cans, rubbish, urine-smelling newspapers and cats, I stood in the yard maybe six feet long with a stinking toilet one end. The moon seemed cold and distant, and I thought, fuck it, you're mad, you're having a good time aren't you? What do you want anyway?

Drones of 'with the Memphis blues again' floated through a window and I went back inside.

Ruby was sitting wryly on an orange crate while the guys talked about dope scenes, freak outs and mushies. Tony was maybe eighteen, already been busted, and living off the dole. The house was dirty, walls painted black and hung with torn posters. They were living in this dump and finding it 'groovy' having come from easy middle class backgrounds.

Naturally I ended up in the basement in Tony's wrinkled bed. We undressed each other slowly like sleepwalkers and I was telling myself I wasn't at all nervous, it was only logical I'd feel a little peculiar, the first man after John and all that, it wasn't familiar, it was a stranger.

Tony was skinny and pale and ducked under the covers before I really saw him. So I lay down and stroked him and we peered at each other anxiously, I made him wait, I made him slow himself down, it was crazy to be impatient.

We rolled around on the bed in that dingy ugly basement. You'll get rheumatism, I said, living in such a damp room. It's cool, he said, as I felt John flowing away from me, melting on the narrow mattress. There was nothing to be said in the basement as dark as a hole in a stocking. We shared a sticky cigarette and he fell asleep almost immediately.

I lay there thinking things like, there it wasn't so difficult was it, admit it was damn good, god you can be a defeatist sometimes, this single life is okay. And I congratulated myself ... on what? this single bed and one cup of coffee reality, this free agent, no responsibility ...

Just before dawn I dressed and left the house so Tony wouldn't wake up in the morning and wonder who we were. Walking down an alley, things had got themselves together. Okay. The sun was coming up. Streets led into streets.

# Dialogue in Shade

It's about love, he said, leaning on the bar. What are you doing about it, what about that man of yours?

A man becomes weak when he's in love.

Then what about a woman?

Love is a woman's natural state, he snorted, she doesn't change much. But a man is a child when he's in love.

That makes everything easy for you then, doesn't it?

Ah, don't be like that. Only a good woman can stop a man from being weak. Believe me, you got to make it with that man of yours, somebody's got to, there's nothing else.

He poured another drink, on the bar. They floated the backs of their hands in it.

Love becomes killing, it can leave you no shade. It becomes like nobody cares anymore.

I care, if you need it tonight babe ...

She laughed.

Yeah, he said, okay, okay.

You got to try though, there's nothing else left now. Nothing else.

Nothing else.

Surrounded by fish-backed drinking people. Suddenly a woman pushed between them screaming, Rick, Rick I can't stand...

Fuck off, baby! he shouted. My wife, he paused.

# End of the Moon

And she says, standing in a narrow room overlooking a dark street, I just presumed Sam and you turned on ... And turns to you with her pale moon face and you stammer, well I have, I do, I mean ... Sam doesn't, he doesn't need to . . . And she laughs a little awkwardly murmuring doesn't need to, and her face takes on veils and her features seem to dissolve.

She walks through the lounge room into the kitchen to make coffee, and you don't follow her but stop by a wooden cabinet with latticed glass doors, and start opening drawers with little knobs on them like Chinese jewellery boxes, and there are lots of slender necked pipes, different sizes laid out inside the drawers, and down the bottom a glass hookah ... And you sigh and think not again, you've been here before, but then you stop something in your mind and think maybe it'll be different this time, maybe ...

You are sitting in the lounge room with the blinds drawn looking at a bookcase that has about half a dozen books in it, then *Nova* magazines and *Vogue* and *Bazaar* and occasionally a *People* ... And she's sitting on a brown vinyl settee with her moon face staring into space or sometimes her white hands picking bits of wool off her jumper, and you don't feel like talking because the room seems asleep and the atmosphere lethargic, and you sort of feel it'd be an effort to be enthusiastic ... Her moon face is sleeping, her pale face is waiting in a tomb, a mummy ...

Then he walks in thinly with a plastic pouch in his hand, and she makes a vague gesture towards you and he turns and looks at your face and you know he hasn't seen you and somehow you feel cheated ... Then he sits down and there's a dull silence, a lack of energy, not that you don't like silence, you do, but some kinds ... depending on the people who share it ... And he says do you want to turn on? and moon face nods tiredly, it's nothing new and you feel slightly uneasy and vulnerable of course. Then he looks at you with a question or an answer on his face, and goes to the wooden cabinet and selects one of the pipes and undoes the pouch ...

You're thinking how does he know which one to choose? and packs the bowl in dead silence, and you wonder at how expertly he does it, you never did learn to do it well yourself ... And lights up and passes the 'pipe around and when it's your turn you shake a little, it's been long and when you were there before lots of bad things were happening ... And you draw in and suck your cheeks and swallow and hope it's not the beginning of bad things, no, you think they couldn't possibly be repeated, but then you're not so sure and shake every time the pipe comes round, and try to hide your nerves and hope they haven't noticed.

Sam is somewhere up the road giving painting lessons to doctors' wives, and you know it's less than five minutes away to get to him but you feel cut off as if you'd have to swim dark oceans and climb savage mountains, and maybe when you got there he'd be dead anyway o,r not want you anymore ...

Moon face is rocking on the lounge and the guy is just staring mutely into space and then there's a strange feeling between you three, the silence fills with currents, somebody laughs and the three of you are laughing and it's all so secret you've really got some joke on the world, and you can see the laughter rising in small coloured bubbles to the ceiling that looks as if it's made of cake ... And you become one of them, you're a laugh bubble locked inside with your knees drawn up and an invisible circle around. and protecting you ... And you're floating and you've definitely got something on the world and you no longer care about moon face or the guy or running into ... And you can't think of repetition, whether you've been through all this before ...

There are remembrances of black velvet collars with silver leashes in the night leading ... Or velvet hooks which catch your skin and slippery nails that tear at your thighs, and the black is breathing and expanding, your mind filling with the dark that is oh so soft yet frightening to lie back in, your body filling with the long silver needle and the doctor's face becoming a dummy that's trying to pretend it is real, but you lying back and knowing there's nothing behind it, nothing ...

Your lips are blue, the face twitching with colour, the room is filled with flying ants with sharp teeth, grow bigger and sting, and you don't want to be hurt, not after the laughing, no, you don't want to feel pain, that blood rip black ... anymore ...

Where are you Sam, oh there, and you smile at him and try to ask him how his painting students went, and he looks at you kind of queer and says, what's the matter with you? You laugh and say, I'm just in a fine mood, a fine fine mood, and you laugh again and it arches out in a long wobbly taper from your throat, your throat of blood ... And somehow it seems sort of hysterical so you lie on the floor staring at the ceiling and wondering what happened to moon face and the other ... Maybe they're down the street less than five minutes away, and you feel you'd have to climb savage mountains arid swim dark oceans to get to them if you wanted to, and somehow they're so vague now except there was a tomb, a mummy, many bandages, and somehow you don't want to ...

## *Future*

It doesn't really matter if I met him in a bar, picked him up or was picked up; in the morning he pushed me out of bed saying, 'You must go, my wife's due back.' And catching the 7.43 am. bus I thought, it doesn't really matter, what did I expect? These are my fingers spread out to touch, the palms turned down, the kisses like nets; these are the lines, when I was a girl the fortune teller said, 'You will travel.'

# The Treadmill

A picture frame window. The sea behind faded muslin curtains. Out on the headland waves fall back to expose glistening rocks humped together like patent leather shoes. A headland of wet shoes. They don't fit anybody.

Behind the picture window and muslin curtains their thin hands finger each other. The cold bones of the hand from the wrist down, someone's pale hand trying to rub a narrow feeling ...

The hotel was old fashioned, down the coast, and their room (the only guests in the place) was supposedly the best with floral maroon carpet and rickety double bed with a fibre mattress. The bridal suite. Some eighty years old.

The whole place seemed overshadowed by the sea, in every room the agitated waves trembled across walls, crockery in the dining room, carpets; lay flat as a hand on furniture, throwing up bubbles, shapes resembling animals, froth, misshapen dreams.

They washed silently in ornate china bowls with warm water and thin bars of soap, dried themselves watching rain stream down the glass till their thoughts damp and cold ...

'Did you remember to leave some food out for the cat?' Yes, yes. 'And lock the door?' Yes. 'It's so cold I think I'll get into bed and read (there seems nothing else to do), it's pretty dismal isn't it.' Nada took off her slacks leaving her jumper on (again, a bed), shivering as she pulled back the sheets.

Brett paced around staring at the raindrops rattling down the pane, feeling their cold stiffness, smoking nervously one cigarette, another. And looking across at Nada wondering what the hell they were doing here anyway: He hated trips, it'd been her idea, and look at the bloody rain. He pulled his coat tighter wishing he was at home with the cat, with the familiar...

She'd insisted they come, saying it'd be really good for them, that they had some things to sort out properly this time. But something in his head wouldn't come forward. Why come all this way to talk? They could do it at home. And he didn't want to talk, rather read, let things mull over in their own silence. Nada seemed so bored at times, complaining she just wanted to get up and leave, go somewhere else, different, have different responses.

And looking at her she seemed so flat, maybe it was him, he knew he was too. Something like a dull tiredness, something maybe like acceptance or resigning.

It had been raining since they arrived. No chance of walking on the headland, easy to fall off, simple to fall off, give over, let everything go. No. He considered himself much too strong for ... what the hell was he doing, having fantasies a hundred miles down the coast? But floating up just the same. Someone's awkward hand. Thinking feet in shoes that didn't fit. Beds that were adrift, drowning.

A picture frame window. Late afternoon. Still raining. The room was very dark except for a flute of white light where Nada had lit a candle. It could be very romantic, it could be very ... people look beautiful in candlelight, they taste so much ... she lay there dozing, imagining, with her legs spread apart under the covers (he could see their indent), her hands slack along the top. She opened one eye and stared at him then closed it, waiting. And he knew she wanted him, to feel warm, together try that possibility.

He remembered somewhere in the bush, legs deep in grass, but even there trees watch, he remembered, the fear of someone coming, not wanting to force himself ... keeping back, imagining eyes in public places, imagining public eyes in private places. Tentatively. Yes. Not knowing what happens when all control is blown. Tripping when you should be naked. Feeling tested, stripped, exposed. Keeping control, control. Then feeling tested again, laced in.

She was looking at him. Somehow he got there with his clothes off under the covers, holding her but the distance seemed immense, vast awkward domes pushing between them, pressing them further apart. The horror of reaching out to touch and getting your hand caught in a treadmill that keeps on grinding, grinding, mashing you up when you want to scream out and stop, just love each other, love ...

'Oh please do that harder.' Someone's face collapsed along with a body. A woman's breast was lukewarm when it wanted to be hot, a nipple soft when it could have been hard. A woman's mouth was too lethargic to kiss much. A man's thighs felt too obvious. Movements were too aware of themselves. He felt pushed and pressured, unsure under her gaze. She felt vacant under his. Fingers became like teeth.

They touched each other and saw only themselves. What have I done, what has he/she done? What are we? As rain poured down self-fullfilling wells where known things were anticipated.

They got up and dressed silently. Going down the stairs placing one foot then the other, staring as it bends at the end of a leg, knowing it's there but not really feeling it.

In the dining room they ordered drinks, sitting at a table each reflection distorted by shadows, alone, rain washing in isolated drops. And no laughter from the curtains.

# *Stuffing*

Rain falls, as lightly as grated cheese through a sieve. Morning. Boys weld metal with iron torches, their faces blazing behind steel masks. Factories. Men build ships, hammers resounding across the harbour, their bodies sheathed in grey overalls, heavy. Work.

Morning. I could have asked him to take me. Or. I could wash my clothes at. a laundromat instead of by hand. Morning. I could wear fluid make-up to make my skin look an even colour. I could be without any distinguishing marks. Then, as bland as the face of a slug. A platter of sameness.

He said, get up, you must make it to work, we'll have no bread for the rent otherwise. Make it, he said, we can make it only if you work, not me.

He rolled in his striped cotton pyjamas, like a caged animal, his mouth sucking on a six inch joint, a lolly stick, getting it out, getting what he wanted out, leaving half an inch for me ... After all, you don't want to be too high baby, he advised. You kidding? Otherwise they might detect something. Those snoopy gigs ...

I rolled out of bed in a spare pair of his striped pyjamas, the drawstrings half way up my chest. We made siamese twins together, the identical stripes curving in, joining, anywhere but in the head.

The flat was lined with skeleton hands, are they? dark, left over from some other day - I had half an hour to make it to work.

Lunchtime. I waited outside looking at the street buckled like a grey caved-in mouth, and he arrived very sharp in a shot-coloured trenchcoat belted with a Japanese iron. buckle, had perfumed his beard; we supported each other with elbows to Hyde Park, sat under a large tree and smoked a joint each. As the trees turned to leaf waves, I wondered if it'd be better if they'd turned to sandwiches. Lunch. Sandwiches? he queried, no baby, what could be more groovy than this, after all? Perhaps he was right, it wasn't groovy to get hungry. Food was a drag.

After all ... I stared away at the fountain, squirming with liquid arms, showering dome heads, little sun drops for teeth - mouth, smirks, marshmallow fingers, sun hair ... imagining bananas, grapes like soccer. balls, finger buns with icing along the nails, nuts with beetles inside ... but back to the fountain, water fountain, pigeons strutting round the concrete flared skirt, its hard rim.

Moisture and fog, lame birds holding the trees up, branches being crutches, roots being wooden legs ... after all, the sky was packed with down, I could break off massive handfulls, falling between my fingers, crumbling beside my nails.

Scrub my back will you? He rustled water in the tub, yellow water lapping up past his ribs, his body turned amber beneath the surface. I knelt with the soap-on-a-string, some special kind he preferred, and rotated the oval till foam spread from its sides, like when you step on a snail and crush it, the insides spilling out sidewards, across your path.

His back turned to a mountain of foam, *blancmange,* popping and crackling in my ears, clogging the water, turning it cream. He grunted with soapy satisfaction, steamy bath pleasure, and shifted his weight, flattening one buttock, then the other; and little coils of black hair curled up from between them like giggles.

That's enough now baby, so baby dropped the soap down its string, and left him soaking.

Morning. And morning glory twines past the window, purpling mouths with splayed mauve fingers extended out. Those thin mauve fingers bulbing with headaches - taking a hundred seeds and mixing them to paste, or eating them as they are - at fourteen, the whole school eating seeds, trying for a high after reading about it in the Sunday papers. The warning that was given, of what not to do, and everyone trying, walking round with headaches, fuzzy zigzags of colour in the brain, stitched needles.

A tin fence leans to, orange, yawning, patched and dented. Morning. The mind jerks from one spring to another, leaping and twisting into memory.

Coffee, baby? he put my feet up on a chair. Get paid? he leaned towards the wrinkled bag. I straggled a hand in my lap, pulling bits of hair off, feeling my stomach push out like a blind face - think, think, get this clog out, too much dope, too much, I can't think, my brain is so heavy.

And the stomach, what is it, appendicitis? Blind skin face giving out flashes of pain. I started to tell him but he said, pain? pain's groovy. Groovy! Everything's groovy. I don't believe it. Something's wrong.

You're not cool, he was filing his soft nails in a corner. You must get cool, baby. But will it stop? ... I can't ... my heavy ... stop, not tonight ... can't you tell ... wrong ... pain is groovy ... now now, oh, he is an easy lover, gone so quick, he is bored with it - every night, like some people read the paper or listen to the news - nothing but habit; grass is better, he says, never waste your high on sex ... that's nothing ... I am his bed machine, he is my lawnmower, I am of no special significance...

He used to run five pros before, and Carol, with her floss cream hair, she wouldn't work unless she was stacked.

But you baby, he'd turned enough times, you look so unnoticeable, I mean baby, shit, no one'd even notice you in a crowd, and yet close up you're okay really. But baby, I gotta be seen with Carol or some other chick, you know, glamorous, the noticing bit - I gotta be seen with a distinguished chick, you dig?

Yes. I want to get to a doctor to cut out this pain. Doctor? doctors aren't cool baby. Shit, the only one I dig is in Melbourne. Relax, here, have a stick.

Like a whirlpool, fragments of memory swirl to the surface; dark brown carpet, striped drawstringed pyjamas, bed with one sheet (on the bottom), dim light, pouch of weed under a carpet square, fifty jazz records, torn covers, texta-colour drawings on the skirting boards, soap string hangings.

For god's sake baby, don't you find this groovy? No, there's... I don't dig routines. Routines? hey baby, cool it, don't black snake on me.

He tossed aside his striped fly and ...

I've had enough baby! You wanna go to a doctor and I told you about

48

them. And now you want me to scrub your back, and bring in some bread. You've really got it twisted baby, all back to front. You wanna see what we're like when we're not high? Oh baby, you're shit. You're so uncool it makes me sick. I'm gonna split this scene baby, but no need to be angry, you can come and make it with me when you're cool. But I can't have a chick who isn't cool, you dig? Sure baby, see you sometime.

There was stuffing pouring out of my legs, or maybe my head - old straw, crushed stalks, broken filings, twisted things.

Doctors? they're so clean and white. I hate white, anything that seems colourless.

A long silver tunnel echoing space walls; groovy ... you must be ... cool . . . be cool . . . baby ... The space tunnel shimmers, memory distortion, buckling in, elongating. A laughing glass tunnel warped and exaggerated, defences, hatreds, confusions. In the silver tunnel where both ends seem to meet, footsteps like stones falling on stone, hard, distorted realities.

Morning. The rain has ceased, the sieve has been blocked and taken away. Morning. And birds still sing, whistling fluffy tubs. The rusted fence yawns and shuts its mouth, leans in near the window, its patches closed.

# The Relationship

## One

She was adrift in her repression, afloat in her sealed fear, and she said, he might chop off my head; he needs psychiatric help.

I couldn't be bothered talking.

Nineteen letters he sent her, all insults; nineteen times she's decided to retaliate might be dangerous.

What's this? Fear sprouting like cauliflowers from her eyes, her knuckles, her mouth - nineteen times of evasion.

There is this fear of men, she feels, they might chop off her head - men are dangerous, she said. Nineteen letters of attack, and she's taken them all lying down; nineteen times - to break through, yet she's refused.

*Two*

She is mad, he said, you know that don't you? Ever since we met she's done nothing but snipe at my personality, he sniped. I am giving her up; she needs psychiatric help, he said. Nineteen times I've tried to help her, broaden her mind but it's useless; all women are mad.

At the age of nineteen I couldn't be bothered talking to them. I've had women, he said. I've travelled this green planet and discovered the world is stupid. And women are the same. They all want to change me - and she, she's done nothing but snipe at my personality.

And his tongue became a wasp and glowed orange with the sting; and the black stripes on the wasp's wings banded his mind and locked him in.

*Three*

A thick mist glides down and clings to his gloom.

At the masonite factory he pushes boards into a machine, levels them till their surfaces become smooth.

He levels and stacks, he levels and stacks. All women are mad - he hates as he stacks - they all want to change me. He smoothes his reason back until it's that of a child's - I've travelled the world and discovered it's useless: there's too much sun in Afghanistan, not enough quiet in Tibet, too much fog in England; and women are mad and everyone is stupid.

He pushes the boards into the machine. I am alone - and in this he takes consolation. I am superior - he wallows. I've suffered for years, yet I'm still here. His pride swells with the ...

He smoothes and stacks, he smoothes and stacks. The factory bristles with accusation, in every corner among the shavings he finds a new loop hole - I am superior - alone - I have suffered - I have to live with peoples' ignorance. SUPERIOR. I AM SUPERIOR. I'VE READ THE GREEK CLASSICS. The factory echoes now with reassurance.

He is mad, his fellow workers whisper.

### Four

Hold on, hold on. I must keep to the rails, she tells herself. I've never met a decent man, they all want to dominate me. I'm sick of their egos.

She turns this ancient habit over in her mind.

I've tried my best with him. Cooked him nice meals, washed his underwear. I sewed his buttons and tried to humour him when he came to me full of despair. I've been good to him. But he'd never see anything my way; always treating me as if I'm inferior. And now he sends me nineteen letters saying, like all women I'm irrational, and if only I'd done what he said, and changed, we would have ...

Now I realise he's dangerous, and my instinct was right - all men are mad.

### Five

There is a train, something phantom and loose in her mind, but strong enough to hold, the wheels are greased.

My marriages have failed - always the same. And with him it's no different; the talking down so I'm afraid to speak; his taking for granted my cooking meals, just because we're lovers. And he's convinced he's superior. I could tell him one day, I could really tell him, just once I'd ... but he's mad and could be dangerous. Why should I suffer at the hands of madmen?

I have enough problems. I am alone.

## Six

You know she's stupid, you know she's mad, he said. I've done my best for her - tried to show her the right path, to broaden her mind, make her more aware. But it's useless, she's like everyone else. She refuses to think.

And she's done nothing but try to undermine my character. All women are the same - they want to change me.

At nineteen I couldn't be bothered.

I have tried, she said. I have endured, he said. You'll understand when you're older, they said.

## Seven

Cauliflower fears and misted despair.

I've never insulted anyone, she says. I've tried to enlighten many people, he says. They will go on a journey together, on their separate rails.

Somewhere a train rattles along narrow lines, lamps sway as it lurches, old ghosts fill the walls. The multi-faced driver is fixed like a wooden puppet to the wheel; the sliding landscape on either side bursts into colour, plants like lush sentinels beckon in the vibrant air, birds throw notes like pebbles at the shadowed windows - the train does not stop, but rattles on, in fixed motion.

# Saturday Night at the Local

Under the neon glare of infection the pub crawls infested with the burns along someone's arm, along the length of the wet bar. Tonight you're nobody repeating the nobody of yourself, in so many ways, drink it down, drink, somebody's shouting, somebody's ordering the wet drink to cum altogether commonly known as pleasure.

This is your pleasure at the end of the week, somebody's beginning to blow it all, or sleep it off, or maybe arrive the morning after at the bottom of your head.

'Honey you're so lovely, let me kiss your hand, your arm, let me kiss the inside of your head, your arse. Are you going to the party later at 177? I'll see you there.'

'But he's a cunt you know, he didn't have to do it that way. He could've just told me straight!' a girl is shouting, 'He didn't have to bring her to our house, he didn't have to be fucking her in my bed did he? I mean, it didn't have to be that brutal did it? He could've just told me and I would've left, I would have really! It didn't have to be that way ... I mean ... brutal ... '

Somebody buys her another drink, but she's raving and screaming, 'What's happening to us all? We're falling apart, he didn't have to do it that way. I went berserk, I just freaked and started smashing things and somehow I got out of there and rushed around to Jenny's and dumped some of my things there, and came down here. I just freaked, that's all. She was so ugly, he was fucking her and she was so ugly ... '

A weedy looking Scottish guy in a dark brown suit is ordering a beer, 'This sure is some kind of pub, I've heard all about it - all these hippies. Wow it really swings, I'll definitely come here again. (maybe I'll get to go to lots of parties, even get off with some wayout hippie bird, try some of that marijuana stuff, oh boy, oh boy) Wait till the fellas at work hear about it, all these weirdos ... '

Three hours later, the Scottish weed swaying with one hand round a schooner, the other clutching a string of beads hanging from someone's neck, 'Listen mate, I really have been overseas and stopped off in India for a couple of days. Well no 1 didn't get to have any of that pot but I had a really wild time 1 can tell you,' clutching and swinging on the beads, 'Hey listen, listen do you know where there's a party? Are you going to a party, are you?'

The guy wearing the beads is wondering how to get rid of this creep - he's really got hold of his beads. 'Alright alright, there's a party at 177 Rose Street, yeah that's right, but I've got to split now,' taking off his beads and leaving them in the Scot's hand.

At ten past ten the footpath outside is jammed. The Scottish weed is shouting and flashing money around. He spots the guy who left the beads with him, 'Hey I'm giving it away,' throwing some notes in his face, 'I want you to have it, you're my friend, it's all yours. I know you hippies don't have much money, and I can afford it.' He throws some more notes around him.

'Listen man, I don't want your money, I don't need it.'

'But I want you to have it, you must have it!' He's screaming and red in the face, 'Listen you bloody bastard, if I want to give you money I'll bloody well give it to you! You're a friend aren't you? And I can give money to a friend, that's right isn't it?' He has a Popeye grip on the guy's arm.

'Yeah sure man, sure,' the guy picks up the notes and puts them in the top of his suede boot. The Scottish man flings an arm around him and they lurch off in the direction of 177.

The girl is still screaming, 'He didn't have to do it!' as someone drags her into a car.

A wave of seething bodies lurch along the streets. The rest leave in cars, driving over broken bottles and glasses.

# Wired Out

## Part One

He'd come in asking to see some prints of Michelangelo, some line drawings of male nudes - that was okay, she'd opened a folder and started going through, but no, not drawings of buildings or Italian ladies with flowing bosoms, he wanted the male nudes in drifting poses, legs out-stretched, open, or better still a couple of them, together with their arms and bulging muscles; she'd laughed and he'd come closer saying you know, you get what I want, don't you - nudes, male ones. But it was no good, the poses weren't erotic enough, they were too formal; she opened a Da Vinci folder - was that better? He grinned and she could feel him warm. But they couldn't find anything suitable. He wanted to get one blown up, to be hung above his bed - you know, his double bed with the velvet cover and black sheets that showed up so good against a person's skin, that made it so much starker and visual - you know.

He came in some weeks later when she was tired and living in a room as big as a toilet closet at Darling Point, the rent so high and the place with a bed, a dresser, wardrobe and chair, there being just enough space to stand between the dresser and bed, about three feet, near the window made of louvres with wire over the outside. He was sharp looking but conservative, always in a dark blue suit and white shirt, his black hair Brylcreamed back, thin gold-framed glasses. He was Lynne, that's what he said, and he always carried a perfect and expensive gold lighter, with his hands neatly, manicured, taking it out to light his cigarette; and his face and skin so clean and shining, unlined, almost the face of a boy ...

They went for coffee next door to Anna's work, and it was understood she sat in the corner seat and he pressed his legs next to hers and laughed and rubbed her thighs occasionally; lighting two cigarettes, one for her, with the perfect gold box between his smooth fingers. At first they talked about Michelangelo, his drawings of beautiful men with their full biceps, overdeveloped organs, and he liked to hear about paintings, though not having seen too many himself, mainly male nudes, Da Vinci - he'd been looking for years for the perfect body caught on white paper, the perfect line he could lie in bed and warm himself with when he was without a lover. Always Lynne buying her coffee, telling her of his latest, what new pleasure he'd invented. Other times when there was no waiting man to be picked up in the Men's, he'd go with lesbians, who wanted to be used like men anyway; and then there was always Kim, a very heavy twelve stone butch with a bleached crewcut, who'd rub cold cream on his stomach and legs all over till he was warm and sticky, 'She's very large on the cream, honey,' and they could turn and slither eely with pleasure on the black sheets.

Up, up, Anna twisted in the cold sheets at night in her room dreaming of a man with the right kind of ... buds exploding ... take her out of the closet, the one corduroy skirt and faded flannel blouse, the broken bra straps ... and no fears of being jumped with no one to help when there was crying and moaning and something tearing at your clothes forcing you down the hitting and blood under the lips the river and salt knowing there was nothing to be done but clean up the ... and ...

Out, out, the legs getting up every morning, the ten cent bit in the slot, the burnt toast and cold shower; seeing the other tenants in the communal eating room downstairs where there was nothing but furtive glances: 'Have you finished with this gas jet? Can I borrow a cup of flour to make pancakes, I'm all out of money? God is that all you've got? I can see you're broke too ... ' Ha, ha, where's the meat, the vegetables, the drawers of soft underwear, perfume smelling like dried leaves to make you smell good, feel good, where's the ten cent bit, where's the man, the flat, the money, the shit ...

Jan came sometimes to give her a joint to make her high to make her feel better; and she could sit around in a red crocheted dress with a bag full of what makes you feel good and get away from what is or isn't real or hell. Jan was making it, she had ... what was it, the right kind of? ... given over, security? Coffee at the Piccolo, records, no work, money. Jan had food, perfume, underwear, Gauloises, knowing, making, making it, make ...

Lynne came once, maybe twice a week to give Anna cigarettes or lunch: 'To make you eat so you'll look better honey, you could look better but I know there are hang-ups, twenty dollars a week ... ' There isn't much else besides the skirt and sandals - toes grow chilblains.

A few times they went to dinner in a coffee bar: mushroom omelette, buttered toast; and his silly kinky legs pressing on hers, not trying, just funny; and his lighter and melon face ... He'd spend hours every morning showering and perfuming his arms and neck, legs, he never forgot his legs, and cleaning his teeth twice for that perfect ring-of-confidence white smile and Brylcreaming his head and polishing his glasses ... There was cutting into pizza pies, Lynne saying: 'More, do you want more - have some cake, ice cream, more coffee, after-dinner mints, what do you fancy, licorice allsorts this week or toasted marshmallows?' They'd go to Darrell Lea's to get sweets, sugar for you, for you dear, to keep it going, the weeks, the hours, to keep the legs moving and the eyes watching the men you serve, the prints they buy - science fiction, surrealism, books on films, Garbo's stone face, the perfect shroud or ...

Each man so different, or all the same? Each head and body, arms and those mouths - all the conversations that could lead that could ... who did it? Have you finished that book you bought last month? I remember when you last came in, something, who did it, did he kill her in the end, was it Agatha Christie or did Thomas Mann drown himself in a German river? I've never read Thomas Mann. Are you married have you kids lollipops I don't care, have you eyes can you touch can you smell the black shroud? Wrap it up, wrap me up, do you wrap yourself? I want to love you I want to hate you I hate you, will you take me out to buy me a coat send me a heart a plastic kiss an I-hate-you card a dead cat a puma's eye - touch me touch ... ha! Ridiculous, you probably want to be touched yourself whoever you are ... I hate you 'cause you're not there ... I'm not here. I want to live with you I don't care if you're ugly we're all ugly, have you a black box do you live in a toilet I have wire on my window you have wire on your window we are all wired out from ...

*Part Two*

Winter. Leaves were shrunken parchments in gutters, legs red and frozen, and there was a need for an overcoat to keep out a need, desire ... Anna was through working, the streets grown black as pupils of giant eyes, and Lynne arrived buttoned in, carrying a bottle of something clear, getting a cab and helping with the door. He came in, this first time, and sitting in her room with his peaked shoes and straight pants, he was appalled at the congested area - they vaguely discussed sharing an apartment at Elizabeth Bay, a modern unit where Lynne could bring his men, and Anna hers if there were ... Sitting low on the bed, he lit with the gold lighter, and it was good now, rubbing her back and massaging her stiff neck, down her cold legs; and she wanted him now, his face, kindness, something. She lay on her front and he stroked her bottom, and she felt uneasy, perhaps he wouldn't turn her, he might. . . She wriggled a little, twisting her head to register with her eyes, not her skin, where his hand was - he seemed contented, cat-like, she turned around, the wine, the atmosphere - he leaned back suddenly saying, it was nice to rub backs but he was tired dear, quite tired, and yes, and with you, but I'm tired, must go, you understand dear.

He left her to drink the dregs, feeling as if he'd never come again to light cigarettes or soothe her neck, he would disappear like the others. It's this damn closet and my damn skirt and damn bitter face ... too hard, and my damn cowardice, building something on the other not myself ... this damn ... lack ... money ... cool ... sickness.

He didn't come and she knew it was more boxes and shrouds, going home to her hole to burrow and burrow and keep herself down. It's been another illusion, but no that's too easy, perhaps next week or next, I might have burrowed so far I won't get back to what, wherever, where are you Lynne, something?

*Part Three*

It couldn't be true. Coming back from lunch there was a gold wrapped parcel, a packet of cigarettes inside a tapestry box, embroidered painting on the front: De La Tour, somebody like that. From Lynne, it said, to you dear from Lynne. Incredible. It no longer mattered if he talked of his aberrations for the rest of eternity, it didn't matter, he was there, she could think of nothing better than to sit and listen to what kinky thing, what pleasurable pain, instrument, excessive ...

She couldn't wait to see his melon face, hear him laughing about a new brand of cold cream, some hotel with a schoolboy, hitting with the braces, wrapping his school tie around his legs; it sounded fine - she was his confessor, the one to listen, to reassure him he was the greatest, the most unique, to never age, forever ...

Rain poured down on her feet and they were cold without stockings, and she was smoking a damp cigarette, waiting under a brassy light; he'd said he would come, bring a bottle, take her home - he'd said he would come and he was late, hours ago, across the sea, she couldn't accept he wasn't coming, he'd be here, soon, just another hour, ocean, or three or four, she was waiting in the rain with damp smokes and drenched ... To come so she could forget herself, just forget the shrouds and boxes and Jan not having been round for weeks; it was raining and all the clocks were laughing at her because he hadn't come, and the town hall clock was just chuckling just roaring with ugly laughter just.

The closet was freezing and she lay smoking in bed, leaning out her arm to ash on the dresser. She'd hidden the alarm so she couldn't see the time, and rain was pouring down in ugly tears against the wire, it was beating on the wire, she could feel it trying to get in and drown her, fill her bed till it sank into the harbour. Cold was eating into her skin, filling it with ice spikes, jabbing, piercing, holes gaping ... through the spikes she heard knocking and got up pulling on a stretched singlet. He was grinning with a huge bottle under his coat, glasses glistening, apologising, she didn't care, there was room to dry off on the bed, open the hysteria; he'd even bought two wine glasses with stems that seemed to be growing; gulping wine and laughing at nothing, the bed warm now, afloat.

There was wine spilled on the sheets; he rubbed her back, smoothing his hands over the singlet, the room filled with giggles; all over, his hands and face, her feet and legs, down her back sliding the stretched ribs, on her skin her body melting the ice spikes, alive ... he turned her and was in bed, white skin and hair like an oiled cap, his glasses on the dresser with the ash, turned her face saying what funny little breasts, funny, for once she wasn't self-conscious, they were eyes and winking, he wasn't making fun of them. He had hardly any hair on his legs and even the toenails were tailored. There was no crushing but a softness, a web, of hands and shoulders a placing of skin, and meeting, entering her, a shaking sea, a split sky, spreading the web, expanding across the room, filling the walls, a web sticking going on through her belly, and clinging on her face, wet trails down her thighs ...

He went before morning, and some weeks later there was coffee and cigarettes, hearing him talk again of his cold cream, bell boys, men's rooms, calling her dear, if she'd met a man yet ... moving away from the closet, a new job, once she met him up the Cross and he was living with someone from Les Girls, and she'd met a man, and he just laughed patting her bottom.

# Future? You Must Be Crazy

These days are getting crazy. The moon blots out the clouds as the astronauts promote Coke. He says, don't worry about the future, there's no way you can tell what's going to happen. She nods in agreement and lights another joint. There's Sarah Bernhardts all over the streets, walking afghans with golden fur. There's Che and Maynard G. Krebs - every bereted, bearded, button-toting man's in Levis. There must be some way out of here but every room has four sure walls. The streets are covered in dogshit, the council's complaining of noise. Nobody talks sense anymore, it's long since gone into hysteria. The feeling of embarrassment when the Prime Minister appears on television looking like a Chicago gangster. Nationalism? You're crazy. He's reading his speech from a card. There's talk of parties and cheaper dope rates. There's anger at the rise of beer prices. The man in the delicatessen wants to sell more caviar. He's displaying pigs' trotters with little hairs on them, wrinkled prunes and pressed lambs' tongues. He can't understand why his customers think he's a worm, he's just doing his job. He's selling Drive for $4.95. And a traveller tells me it cost him nothing to live in India. He just stopped eating for two years. And then this junkie writes a book about his cure and spends the royalties on junk. It helps him write, he says. Now she wants a triple pernod. The hotel manager wants the rock band to turn down their sound, and wear matching blue shirts. The groupies just want to be loved. They're doing it in pairs, it's less hassle and saves time. Joe's trying to sell some acid to buy himself some breakfast. Fred's dancing on the table. There's knife throwing at John's, they're having a quiet card game. The eat's in the fridge, somebody gave him speed and he's trying to be cool. The goldfish are zonked on Mandrax and trying to eat their plastic rocks. They're breaking pool cues at the pub because it's a serious game. She's quoting A. E. Housman and expecting to get a laugh. Crazy? Who me? I'm going to the fancy dress as a beer carton.

# Steve and the Big Smoke

She has a long pale face, a stringy basin haircut of disputable colour. 'Hi man, got a j?' at any concert in the foyer she's hustling, at the showground, the Art Students' Ball. 'If all these cats put in a buck each they'd have some gear and I'd have some lunch. Where's the love generation gone man? Once I had dope laid on me wherever I went, these days you can't even get a j.'

I could unravel dialogue like a flag and wave it in your face like some kind of evidence ... Insist it's the facts, but I'm no reporter...

Nobody quite could take away that face with its fine network of lines, those bright feverish eyes shifting thorns and veils, the pointed tongue eternally licking dry lips. I could sculpt the hands into plaster bookends, copy the wrinkles on her palms and tough bitten fingernails. Someone could steal the body and freeze it into wax - those pear-shaped breasts or a thousand reflections of Maillol hips. Dress it in jeans, boots, tight leather belt, Vincent de Paul shirt, authentic Spanish hat. She could be erected as the man she was, complete with unwashed hair and furry eyebrows. She could be cruelly derided for her condition - the lack of paint on her face, the discolouring of her eyeballs, the scar on her cheek.

Oh maniac photographer you can be so false.

Oh Madame Tussaud you should be boiled in your own wax.

I'll call this lady Steve and you'll know it's fictitious, but maybe you'll see her in top hat at a demonstration scoring some good acid, or hiking across the Nullabor, the only person in sight, offering you a joint then striding off into the dust. She has a habit of temporarily borrowing/stealing cars when she needs one. Had a black FJ called Thunderbolt, drove it like a horse, in suede waistcoat and borrowed riding boots. Has a habit of running out of tobacco and having to smoke some of her deals. 'It's all one big smoke to me man,' commenting on her thirty-five year life. Has a habit of eating a slice of bread in every house she visits - 'It's less hassle, they can spare a bit of bread can't they?' And there's hundreds of houses - every head from Byron Bay to the south coast. Her basic possessions are a man's silk kerchief, a water tankard and sleeping bag. There's not much to own.

'What do you want that for?' she asked me one day, pointing to an ancient rusted dock I'd found.

'I just think it's beautiful.'

'That's no beauty man, that's history. Been dead and gone, long since ticking. It's served its purpose, why preserve it? It's ugly man, it's junk. You want junk?'

And I had no answer.


'You want to have sex?' she asks me one night, sitting in my room smoking her little roaches. 'I want to make love to you. You want love from me?'

I'm thinking, I like this woman but I don't want sex with her. I say, 'I'm happy with men Steve, I get what I need. I don't *need* to go to bed with you,' feeling like a heel passing back her roach.

'It's not a need is it, it's love ... isn't it?' she looks away warily. I feel like a creep and have no answer.

She's sitting in my room rolling joints as thin as fingernails, producing miraculous roaches from her pockets, sitting crosslegged as a Hindu, her long tired face half hidden under her hair, sitting there like a rock eternally waiting and saying, 'I want to make love to you, I want to touch your body like I touch your mind - that's Cohen - he's said a few things. I didn't think you were straight. Do these men bring you love or just sex? Don't you ever want a woman? Is it more sexy to have a man kiss you than me?'

And I'm offering a million justifications.

I'm not camp.

A woman can't satisfy me like a man.

I'm a hedonist in search of the least limiting pleasures.

My body is made to hold a man not a substitute.

It's quality I'm after.

My mind is female.

My love seeks its opposite.

Etc. Etc.

'You must still think it's wrong to love your own sex,' Steve's saying. 'Your body can hold anything ... like your mind. Maybe you dig sex first, not love?'

Mmn.

I could write an ode to Steve.

Because of the fact she's butch.

Because she's a thief.

Because she's been a junkie.

Because she's a pacifist if possible.

Because she's an orphan.

Because she's tried every drug.

Because she can look beautiful.

Because she plays guitar better than Slim Dusty.

Because she collects young boys.

Because she's an institution.

I don't know if any of these things are important or relevant. The fact she's been in jail. The fact she can't be trusted. The fact she believes in anarchy and is a threat to herself. And these words could be a short story, a villanelle or a delusion. I wonder if Steve would think I've written the truth. I've no idea what the truth is, or if this is secretly a love letter. I'm not a hippie, a junkie or a lesbian.

Steve is a lonely woman with high blood pressure and fucked up kidneys. She's already had a heart attack and probably won't live long.

She's a pessimist, a battler and an anachronism. Her acid punch has real fruit in it. 'Happiness? It's all one big smoke to me, man.' She'll smoke her joint till the end.

## A Part Dialogue About Wrappings

Wrap
Wrap
Wrappings

It's not by my design, said the spider devouring the fly.

But what of this mantis feeling:
if you feed off me I will turn and destroy you?

    Tenderly they embrace
knowing they will never
      commit themselves to each other.

    Wrapped in emotional defences
(I want to remain entirely self-sufficient, etc.)
      revolving through the dark
of their lusts and self-indulgence ...

    They drink and turn on/off
the stone slaying them like mythical dragons,
      roaring, plundering each other's bodies,
passion being the closest they come to love ...

    Through a tear in the wrapping
they touch at vulnerability, recoil quickly,
      the innocent gets burned.

It seemed the only thing to do, said the mummy, uncoiling from his
wrapping and stepping into the other world.

The package would not reveal its contents until someone ripped the wrapping off.

    It's difficult, they were heard to say,
trying to see
        through such a small aperture.

These wrappings are extremely interesting, said the psychiatrist, poking at a pool of tears…

## Vous Voulez?

How many times to wake up with a dull craving in your chest, somewhere the very bottom of your self is struggling up towards a morning - another morning, another day, struggling up from the labyrinth, curving out towards the window, pulling the curtains, drawing the blinds saying - again - as the day floods into the room across the crumpled bed, the fragile boat still floating after last night's storm, the intimate wrestle? How many times? how long it is.

Paris. A small chink of sunlight was trying its face over the curtain rods as Maria opened her eyes. The long brown drapes hung like thick hands over the window, shielding the light from the room, from her body, her sore eyes. She moved sideways in the sagging bed into a smooth hairless shoulder, pale as porcelain - Jacques' shoulder, Jacques.

God, she could hardly bear to look at him, this stranger she'd picked up at the carnival, that she'd ended up with here in this musty cramped flat somewhere in Paris, with Patricia in the next room with Jacques' friend Christian. Christian and Jacques? She lay covered in sweat, cum and dust between two filthy sheets, with nothing to say to him, this pretty little Frenchman looking for someone to marry. Damn it! Ridiculous! Patricia and herself old enough not to be of interest to them, old enough not to be this shallow. Predatory? When she couldn't even speak French, had spent the night giggling with Jacques over red wine, hiding behind her hair and slang like some half-baked fourteen year old, gurgling' Oui oui' to everything he said.

She turned again in bed angered by this flood of recrimination, this necessity to do and undo, smooth the wrinkled picture free of flaws and splinters, smooth the event into a tapestry of illusion, exaggeration, manifestations - these unwashed idols of pleasure, these assassins of decadent destinations; over and over the hand held out in offering to be rejected, consumed, ignored; to reach out and touch a shoulder to find the reflection not satisfying, not fulfilling to the patterns in your self - to find another separate and wrinkled picture, torn and unable to be eased.

They'd gone to the fair, two girls on a holiday in Paris, to mingle with thousands eating croissants, hot dogs and candy floss, drifting from bar to bar, sitting in darkened tents listening to violins and cellos, being thrust pamphlets for the Communist Party (what *is* a Communist?), tickets for the Ghost Train, tickets for the Wild Cat. They'd never been to such a huge carnival. A circus of families with screaming children, old ladies in black crepe hats with red lips and large noses; a sea of denim shirts, silver studs, limbs and handbags, voices rising in waves to the pitch of deafness, cicadas, cicadas, the shrill tide of pleasure.

They'd stumbled across Jacques and Christian fishing, amid a huge crowd gathered round a lit up tank where trout swam crazily between baited lines. They were both brandishing lines, half drunk and nearly falling into the tank. The, girls moved closer trying to figure out what was going on - trout fishing at a carnival? Christian whirled around dripping water on their shoes, 'Good fishing!' he yelled, pulling at one of their arms. Suddenly a trout fell twitching at their feet, its mouth gasping for air. The boys were delirious scrabbling round their legs, grabbing at scales and ankles. Shouts of *'Je ne parle pas Francaise,'* as the trout and girls were carried off into a cafe next door, to watch the gutting and frying of the fish. Ah the French, always thinking of their bellies.

More shouts of *'Oui oui,'* and *'Vin rouge,'* as distortions of conversation broke out between the boys and Patricia (who could speak a little French). Then a maze of tunnels dotted with wine glasses, wind through their hair as a huge spangled ferris wheel lifted them into the sky, swinging them high over the fair, they could see the lights of Paris, quivering and glittering anenomes. It must have been miles walking, Maria could remember feet aching in stupid clogs, Patricia leaning on Christian's shoulder tossing off flashes of happiness and abandon - and why not?

The boys worked together as clerks in the public service, were handsome, moustached, dressed in jeans and short jackets, hair layer-cut appropriately, anticipation? and why not? They fell exhausted into a bar and ordered some more wine. A negro waitress undulated towards them, her white teeth bright as razors, her lips scarlet. She had a short haircut like a man, greased down over one pencilled eyebrow, and wore a dress of brilliant blue cut diagonally from one shoulder to the breast, with only one long sleeve - something a clown might wear, something perfect for a fair.

She thrust one bare black shoulder into Christian's face, 'Vous voulez?' He grinned madly into two black mink eyelashes, Jacques was pushing closer to the bar, not to be left out. A rapid conversation went into action with much eyebrow raising, hip rolling, bangle jangling, eye flashing. Maria and Patricia stood back smiling at the long red nails with gold stars painted where the moons would normally show, the huge gold earrings swinging perilously close to the shoulders, the shimmering nipples glowing through the dress. Fabulous. The negress was jerking her thumb at them speaking in studded English. 'Are they Americans? You found them here of course.' Then running live coals over them. 'But this one has freckles,' staring at Patricia, 'And this one has crooked teeth.' Then she was gone down the bar stretching off into a blur of redfaced drinkers. 'The bitch!' they all laughed. 'She works in a club, you know, strip-tease,' Jacques was telling Patricia in French. 'She likes money,' and they all laughed again, the girls nestled into the boys' shoulders with their bad teeth and blotchy skins.

It was past midnight, they were drunk, they staggered to the nearest Metro, it was closed, they started walking into Paris. Patricia was walking ahead with Christian and Maria could hear her voice floating back, 'Please don't, not here, not in the street, I don't like it ...' and then mumbling, with Christian trying to kiss her as they stumbled up the road. And she had her first feeling of sadness as Jacques squeezed her hand. 'Will you come back to Christian's flat?' It was too late to go back to the hotel, the doors would be locked, and the night had mapped its own course.

The building was very old and dirty, they had to tiptoe past the concierge's room, up six flights of stairs onto a tiny landing. An odour of unwashed dishes, clothes and Gauloises enveloped the girls as Christian opened the door. Then they were sitting in a tiny room with faded rose wallpaper, a blackened gas heater in one corner, an enormous mahogany dresser covered in ashtrays and all sorts of junk. Jacques and Maria sat on a sagging divan, and she couldn't help noticing how grey the sheets were, that when they sat a cloud of dust rose up from the covers, that the table had a grey blanket over it covered in coffee stains.

And Christian and Jacques sat there in their jeans and body shirts, each wearing a silver chain bracelet with his name engraved on it, each embarrassed by the flat, piled on top of each other, rolling their eyes, making jokes. It was ridiculous, sad, what else could clerks afford? In a city as expensive as Paris, with everyone wearing new clothes before anyone would even look at them - the bourgeoisie strutting on boulevards with white poodles, platform shoes, immaculate haircuts - the bourgeoisie sitting in cafes sipping pernod at one pound a drink - the bourgeoisie clanking in gold chains, snakeskin boots, checking it out in Maseratis, trying to make it in Citroens, on the streets checking each other out. For the first time Maria realised they'd probably cleaned the boys out of their entire pay packets - though she'd paid for some of the drinks, what about the Ghost Train rides at five francs each time? the chocolates? the cab fare?

She stared at the old walls, Christian had taped up a few posters of Led Zeppelin, Alain Delon, Tina Turner, etc. She could see the tape stuck across the wallpaper pulling the colour off the rose petals, the windowsill thick with dust, the bidet positively black. She asked to have a shower, to wash off the grime from the carnival, but both of them tried to put her off. Was it absolutely necessary? why didn't she have one at her hotel in the morning? Finally Christian threw her a grey towel and led her into the kitchen. The tap pulled out on a hose, he removed the dishes from the sink. Laughing and joking he left her to stand in the sink, face up to a clothesline that ran from the heater to the wall, to shoot water across the floor showering pots and pans, hose in one hand, soap in the other.

And she could hear them playing records, the sound of Patricia laughing, click of cigarette lighters, unfamiliar yet familiar sounds floating across another night, across a chain of remembered nights and past encounters, more unfamiliar hands on her body, words whispered into ears, thighs pushed towards her struggling to be relieved - the insistent ebb and surge of a million nights, parties, faces, bodies rubbed together under blankets, dirty sheets from other couplings, desperate orgasms going off into darkness; voids, voids, whole rivers of kisses not remembered, of significant words lost in isolation, of the continuity of nothing continuous; fragments and illusion, rising up wave upon wave to be drowned in a sea of emptiness, nothing consolidated or claimed, nothing to fill you up to the point of bursting, of saying, 'Enough! I am satisfied! My desires are sated forever. For once I will not go down into that labyrinth of half-drugged euphoria, desires that are never realised, consumed, resurrected to the point of peace.' To be always needing and asking, tempting with a million tentacles surging into multiple selves, rippling out seeking completion, an end, an end to the sadness of surviving.

So you're still here, always on the brink of another discovery, another voyage - or is it? Is it really digging the treasure out, holding it up saying, 'There, I have it, it's mine!' It glows and resolves this tiredness. It is absolute. It is infinite! When you know it can't remain, or else be found standing, rigid, holding a corpse, a dead and finite thing, unable to move again.

O fragments, damn you, damn this restlessness and eternal search. That you drag this body of limbs into strangers who must drive their fears into you, as if to gouge something from you, take away a piece of you, a mirror for themselves - and you doing the same. Is there no conclusion other than death, the absolute one, when it seems like a chain of deaths, each one in order to live? As you drive your cunt towards them seeking recognition, absolution.

The water had gone cold when Maria stepped from the shower. Jacques was outside the door, 'Have you finished? The others have gone to bed.' And clean and old from the shower she moved towards him like a sleep walker, feeling his hot breath on her shoulder, unable to be still. And through the night he struggled towards her, pulling and pushing at her body, nervous and so impatient, crushing her thighs and digging his nails into her back, without once touching her lips. And she was falling down into darkness, away from his fumbling hands, unable to be on top of him, unable to be anywhere but underneath him, them, to calm or guide his burning hands. Unable to be soft or have him see the lips of her body, speak anything to bring them close, feel fused, blissful, explored - anything other than this emptiness. So she was looking into her own dark mirror, seeing her own tired reflection again.

She fell asleep hearing the squeak of the bed in the next room, as Jacques lay there smoking, twisting her nipples as if they were bottle tops. He woke her again and she heard a voice calling out, 'No please, I must sleep, I'm too tired, I can't.' And he was shaking his head and pulling her legs unable to believe.

It was midday when they woke. The long brown drapes hung like thick hands over the window, shielding the light from the room, from her sore body and thighs. Christian appeared in the doorway in red underpants, smoking a cigarette. Jacques sprang out of bed and they went off into the kitchen, talking and laughing excitedly, comparing notes Maria imagined. And she lay there with the smell of cum on her, like some strange beetle potion she didn't know the use for.

# A View of the Map

Back there you stand squat in a doorway holding a photo already become history. We have fallen away from each other - like so many others - as if we never shared intimacies of tongue and bed, through Eastern hotel rooms and European fog. We are separate and fragmented having lost our voices in ideas of ownership.

Does it always have to be this way? Through peaks and hollows of our lives, bringing histories and conceptual futures to each other - struggling and struggling to discover our presents don't fit. It is happening now, these irrevocable wounds we cement our memories with.

Back here you walk towards me on some invisible line that does not join us. I am sitting back stalls having refused to pay the price - when we have not the strength to force a larger space for us to be in. When we no longer know what that space is. And our futures are crossed.

We say we just want to be. When that affects changes in the other you can't foresee. We can't hold on to an image of a separate self yet hope to merge it with another. We have to forgo something. Yet the urge to seek the other is as crucial as a shadow. We want to be - together and apart.

Perhaps you have found something more than this. When I could not be lover, conversation, life style, television, breadwinner - and still be myself. I could not be past, present and future while I remained in the present with you. Yet isn't this what I do with myself? There is always this confusion.

Back there, in here, further on - there is this map we traverse though we have different means of doing so. You must believe your map is true. I must believe mine is. Our paddles or vehicles are different and separate. My Iceland is at the centre of this map. Knowing you have visited it and gone. That I am the only permanent resident.

## Mice. In Dreams Perhaps.

Plain walls in his room. I think I'll paint the walls almost black. Black. Yes. Drama. Doom. Break up the monotony. He has a ladder by his bed to paint the walls deep almost black. Yes. Sitting there in black crepe slacks impeccably ironed, Italian leather boots. Scottish wool jumper, leather bracelet, leather things, tentative hands. I don't believe in handshaking do you? It's not what I think one ought to do. Do you think? All these formalities. Rituals. Mmn. He moves lightly. Pieces of raw silk rip up the light.

I'm tired of Bunny, I think I'll give him up. Yes? And Clayton is such a bore. Really. He sighs. It's not that sex is hopeless, really, it's just that the more I lose interest in myself, the more I lose interest in it. Got it. It. Tube of emotions. Funnels. And Bunny and I aren't very good in bed anyway. He's rather inhibited, like a squirmy eel wriggling away. I've always thought there was something repulsive about him. He looks so wet! Gasps for breath. I can't stand people breathing on me in bed! God! Suffocation.

He pushes at something invisible in the room. He stands near her lifting his neat eyebrows, meaning to penetrate ... I think the room'd look good painted black. Yes. And yellow sheets'd go well, (that you've never been in) show up the complexion.

They go on. Apart. She lifts her cigarette and he asks her to ash it in a special bottle. I want a bottle full of ash. Nice? And glass jars with coloured water in them, nothing else in the room, a bed perhaps ... Mmn that'd be beaut.

Who's giving who? They lean and fall about the room. Together.

Apart. They can hardly breathe at times, the spaces become so close. So close. At times.

Images poke through her mind, some padding and softly. She thinks of a lover. Someone. Him - the man from the theatre. Kissing her. Unloosing a mouth. Removing clothes and sliding a tongue over an entire body. His ear, openings, releasing - flood of time, movement, around. Another time, awkwardness. Balloons in her mouth. Pushing down. Someone rushing instead of waiting. Needing. Is needed. How much and how little. Need.

Smoking.

Falling.

Riding.

Touching.

Chimes. Unrealised areas. Breaking.


She couldn't go on. Memories are rice paper, crumpling, transparent. Easy if you want them to be.

She was back in the room, having never really left. And Steven was making coffee in the corner, very black, strong. Ears built with honey. Murmuring and fluttering in front of her, over, bumping her foot, she moving the foot away, he apologising, placing the foot somewhere else, drinking coffee, looking away. Some other distance.

Forward. Shuttle of lips and eyes. How's Joel, are you happy with him? Yes . . . she paused to, then looking up - we've had a few flares, oh, anyway, but yes we've been making it okay. Mmn. I guess. She fiddles with her earring, ashes again in the bottle.

And he really meant - is he a good lover? His lips slim. And she thought about it, in the silence. Yes, they'd had some wonderful times together, very ... free? that wretched word ... made things free. She looked up at Steven - there's very few people who are totally uninhibited, if it's possible, I mean most of us have some sexual inhibitions somewhere…

Yes, Bunny's like that. I think I'll give him up. And Clayton's a bore but we're pretty good in bed I think. You know I've realised one can be very good in bed without having to care about it at all. I mean, all this nonsense about love, jerking his leg, it leaves one cold. Cold. There comes a time when one just realises there are more worthwhile things to do, to get on with it. Don't you think? One could spend a lifetime worry-ing about love and such things, and caring, you know, being considerate, when one really ought to get on to the more important things.

He held himself very still, looking at her. She stared deliberately back, then - but Steven I believe in love, I mean I've had some wonderful times with people and it's been because of Joel and me, we've made love till we couldn't move anymore, and that's because of ... love, hesitating, or caring ... move, anyhow, something. Something.

Steven dropped his face. Twiddled buckles on his shoes, flicked bits of fluff off his trousers. And she frowned, thinking we shouldn't be talking about ... I should say ... or ... He crossed one leg over the other, feeling more this, feeling he was not feeling, that she was no more important than anybody else. That all the philosophy he'd read, that. No. He knew she was saying, that she could affect, that ... that there was something, love perhaps? Some closer possibility or reality. Reality?

And then he didn't want Bunny or Clayton or, he wanted ... no! Why should I? I can't stand. No. No. Maybe the sky is, maybe sex is on a level I can't, what is sex?

My boots hurt, my brain is so heavy, I read too much, I am sick of philosophy, I find people gross, I am, I need a new tube of lubricating cream, I am concerned with concepts, I, I must study more logic, more Kant, Mill, Nietzsche, Hegel.

Steven lay in bed smoking a Cuban cigar, making his throat retch - even this, feeling one ought to go in for stronger things, coarser cigarettes, stronger coffee, thicker belts, sweaters, bigger lovers, shoes, blacker clothes, eyes. One ought to do this, one ought to do that. Yes. No. Tedious. Really. How tedious.

He picked up *Beyond Good and Evil* by Nietzsche, mmn, that photo on the cover, he felt a similar likeness, turning his head, had another puff of the cigar, was bored, bored, sighed dropping the book on the floor. Perhaps I should turn on, perhaps I should go overseas, give up sex, improve my body, take up yoga, be a theologian, vegetarian, bisexual, go to elegant parties, give up speaking for five years, thinking. Thinking. How dreary.

Monday he was round again to visit her. Nice. He brought a flower.

She thanked him. Flattered. But he'd already explained they meant nothing to him. And he sat on the bed saying I think one ought to forget about people altogether, stuff them, forget they exist. She listened (as usual) and sighed. No Steven, I don't ... No? I've given up Bunny, he announced, and only intend to see Clayton once a fortnight, for sex. Oh, I don't care, I don't know.

She turned her back and went to the wardrobe to get out a dress. I got a new dress (change the subject). They were aware. Changing in front of him, he watched her body (he hadn't touched), breasts, what were they like? anything, the space between her legs. Do you think it suits me? She liked to show him her clothes, talk about appearances. He complimented her. She was aware. They had hugged once or twice a long time ago. Or had he kissed her on the cheek? She couldn't remember. They were friends. He didn't come on to ...

She hated him sometimes. His selfishness, was it? Or was it herself?

The potential cat and mouse. A devouring. In dreams perhaps, perhaps she only realised it in dreams.

Mmn, it makes you look like Theda Bara. They both laughed, she whirling around in the dress. Some admiration. Mutual tongue licking. And he felt transfixed, staring - legs from cupboards, fingers, crotches, pubic hairs lining drawers, nipples, water. Salt in his eyes - my mind, my mind - he was silently nauseous. Tongues, hairs, sweat, smells, Tongues like whips, hands like whips, words all whips, Ash.

He left the room. And she wasn't concerned, he often did that, rushed off suddenly. She'd never bothered to ask him why. Or think why. Why. He stood on the back steps fitting blocks in his mind, tightening, stoppers in bottles. Held his hands very tight.

Silently, without odours or screaming he walked back into the room.

And sat down again. Begin.

# Cooling Off

Remembrances of blood and hands tying belts in the night light, 500 watt globes, fingers tying cloths, white strips of gauze; in the corridor, legs stitched, bandaids on seats, bandaids on eyes, metal tubes rolling and bumping' through the hospital. Nurse, O nurse with your needlebright eyes, blooming in white with sadist's hands, with bandages inside your head ...

Next morning, this tree now, your petal face broken off, something happens, something not, something gives, something rots ... dry wind off the heat of exhaustion, lift a hand and stir a lemon drink, cool off, and cool off ...

Talk of yellow with hard unmeltable centres, that hard, everything breaks in its own way; across the cricket ground someone is walking, beating balls, cement hands, to get out, into fresh space: Baby, he said, I've been loving and drinking, with fleas in my bed and hands on girls' waists, holding them down like broken lilies, but I'm missing, there's something missing ...

Give over cows and Promite, pills in jars with lids that smell, this joint, this joint earth ... sometimes the ground is so bare, not a green leaf or berry drop, but comes the sun on splinterings, opening nuts, opening wounds; the effort there, the effort lifting up, cooling, off, cooling off - the ground splits and tongues come out red and flicking, then you remember a wheel on bare ground, spokes up and turning on, going round till the ground is filled ...

# It's Just the Full Moon

They hadn't been getting on too well so he'd decided to go to Sydney for a week or two, to have a break. He wrote to Jane telling her he was coming. She was an old friend of his and Sharon's and shared a terrace with a few others in Paddington. There'd be space in the lounge room and he had a sleeping bag.

The trip up in the train was boring and uneventful. He felt tired and depressed. Sharon and he seemed to do nothing but get at each other these days. What did he expect? They'd been together three years now, a damn long time, but the inevitable 'you're so predictable' syndrome was beginning to affect both of them.

It didn't seem possible to live with someone for any length of time without that happening. It wasn't as if he didn't love Sharon anymore, she was still as beautiful as ever, it was this ceaseless repetition of the same old needs, the same tired reassurances given. Nice for the ego to know that no matter what you did someone would still want you, no matter how far out of control you went someone would still know how to handle you. Nice, but castrating. Nice, but boring. He could still take her and fuck her and feel her responding, yet know it wasn't the same; even the body read like a familiar map. It was just the pattern of their lives, knowing what they'd be doing next weekend, knowing who their friends were, where they bought their groceries, how Sharon liked Crumble Bars and getting her back scratched.

He lurched back and forth in the train, angry at having to admit they weren't getting on like they used to. He stared at a woman sitting opposite him in the carriage. She had a tight shrivelled mouth in a slightly grey face. He wondered if she'd ever sat in a train maybe thirty years ago mulling the same problems. But probably if she'd been married she'd stuck to the one guy till boredom had shrivelled her mouth and glazed her eyes. Maybe that was why she was that slightly off-putting colour. He could never imagine Sharon looking like that. But it was useless speculating. Surely he'd feel better after the trip, and it'd be good to see Jane - it always was.

It was absolute streaming sunshine when he arrived in Paddington.

He wandered down a few lanes filled with children, dogs, bicycles and cats' piss. He had the address on a piece of paper. The terraces were extreme - either laced in white wrought iron with pseudo-Spanish archways and convict sandstone, or rotting peeling dog-kennels with warped oak doors, rancid brasswork and pigeon shit on the verandahs. Jane's was the latter so he instantly relaxed.

'You old bastard!'

'God you look magnificent.'

'Where'd you get that waistcoat?'

And there was Jane kissing him, 'How are you, how's Sharon?' looking incredibly good in an Indian kaftan of very bright colours. He sat back smiling, really glad to have arrived. Three cups of tea and two joints later he was definitly glad to have arrived. They decided to go to the pub: he, Jane, Martin and his girlfriend Cheryl, and Dave.


'You're looking really good,' he said, taking Jane by the arm as they walked down the street.

'I don't know why I am, I've been having a terrible time really.' And he laughed rolling his eyes at her, knowing it meant only one thing, her usual traumatic love affairs.

'What bastard is it this time?'

'Well it's all over now, just in the last couple of weeks. I think I mentioned it in a letter, though I doubt if he's worth the postage. He went back to his wife of course. But how are you and Sharon? What've you been doing with yourselves?'

He looked under the tip of her left earlobe. 'Oh fine, we've been getting along okay. Nothing very spectacular happening, just mouldering away, you know.'

And Jane stared at him. Not like him to say 'mouldering', but then she was always too ready to equate her problems with someone else's, or dig them out if they had any.

She couldn't get over how good he looked, being on the dole sure suited him - all that time to cruise around, go to movies, art galleries, read. Though she'd often wondered how he and Sharon got on, spending so much time together, every day as neither of them worked. But Sharon was always cooking, crocheting, making mobiles and things for their crazy room; and they'd been together long enough now, so they should be making out okay. Pity Sharon hadn't come up with him though, it would've been good to see her.

'Why didn't Sharon come with you?' she asked him over beers. 'Oh, she had things she wanted to do. She's not too keen on travelling, can't stand trains, does nothing but complain. Anyway it's hard to get the fares.' And he turned away and started talking to Martin.

By eight pm. they were drunk enough to decide they'd better eat.

Martin and Cheryl had wandered off somewhere and Dave was engrossed in a game of pool.

'Let's go the Greeks,' Jane said, hanging on to his arm.

'Okay, anything you say honey, just lead me on.'

'What's round and orange and travels out of the ground at ninety miles an hour?'

They both collapsed in the gutter. '

An E-type carrot!'

'That's ridiculous, those tired old jokes!'

They bought a bottle of wine on the way, and had much nonsense in the restaurant spitting olive seeds on the floor and shrieking with laughter.

'Oh stop it you drunken bum! You're insane! Whatever would Sharon think of us now?' screamed Jane.

'I don't really care,' he said ponderously, leaning towards her swaying and peering into her eyes, 'as Sharon and I never go drinking.'

She felt that slight pause as she had before, something seemed wrong. It was nothing. He poured her another drink and the rave went on.

By ten to ten he had time to whip into another pub and buy a few bottles of beer.

'I can't possibly drink any more,' Jane laughed, as they slumped back to her house.

'Who says you're getting any, my pretty maid,' leering like a friendly crocodile. 'It's time you changed your ways, leading old boots astray.'

Jane shrieked and supported herself on his arm. It felt good and friendly, even for a crocodile. He flashed a set of beautiful gleaming teeth at her. All the more to bite you with. Ridiculous! She never even allowed the desire to fully formulate. It just flashed by, a lunatic urge.

They sat around the kitchen drinking beer. He'd bought a book of drawings by Escher to show her. There were gardens with magnificent crawling things in them, dragons riding bicycles, gnomes working on strange machines, fat grubs going and coming from work on a stairway that led to infinity. They looked through the book together inventing stories of cockroaches dressed for balls, rats rehearsing for a play, and racoons kissing on screens.

Suddenly Martin burst in dragging a bedraggled Cheryl with him. 'Want to go to a party? There's one on at Edgecliff. We've got a car waiting outside.' And Cheryl just said, 'Oh,' and flopped into a chair. 'I don't really want to go,' said Jane, 'Do you?'

But he decided to go - after all he was supposed to be having a break. 'See you later,' patting her on the head, grabbing two bottles of beer before rushing after Martin and a moaning Cheryl.

She finished looking at the Escher book, wandered round in a daze, cleaned her teeth and went to bed. She dreamed that night of aristocratic lice and negroid toads. In the morning she only found Dave and his hangover sitting in the kitchen. 'Where is everybody?' she asked.

'Martin and Cheryl have gone to see someone, and I don't know where your friend is. I don't think he came home last night.'

She had a look in the lounge room and could see that his sleeping bag hadn't been unrolled yet.

'He must be having a good time then,' she laughed, feeling vaguely disappointed. By what? but again she never let the feeling form into something tangible. It was just good to have him staying, they always got on so well.

He slipped in quietly late afternoon. She was lying on her bed reading a book.

'Hi there,' he called, 'mind if I make a pot of tea?' 'Of course not,' waving her book at him.

He came back a few minutes later carrying two cups, 'What'cha get up to?'

'Oh nothing, went to bed, but I had an incredible dream about negroid toads.' They both laughed. 'What about you?'

'Ah, you might say I got. very drunk and did things I shouldn't have,' turning his gaze away.

And she felt too close to him and Sharon not to feel strange when he said that. She'd always assumed they were faithful to each other, so she couldn't help wondering if he'd done this before. As if it was any damn business of hers. As if people could be faithful after years of being together. Quite unrealistic - she couldn't think of any couples she knew who were, though they mostly did it on the sly. Did Sharon ever know, was it something they ever discussed? She knew Sharon on her part would never be unfaithful - she either ran around unattached or stuck to the one man.

'So long as you had a good time,' she smiled, 'That's what you're here for.' Hypocritical shit. The voyeur's extended tolerance.

'I don't know if I did though,' finishing his tea and leaving the room.


Monday she was back at work carrying plates and capuccinos, smiling as people crammed short blacks and cheese cakes into their mouths, being bored and picking at fluff on her black uniform. That night she bought spaghetti and mince steak on the way home, hoping he'd be there for tea.

He was sitting in the kitchen when she came in, and got up saying, 'How was your day, would you like a cup of coffee?'

She sat down and groaned, 'A drag.'

'Yeah 'most jobs are the same,' he gave her that knowing half smile of his, 'I'd rather be poor and have the time to do what I want.'

When he heard she was making spaghetti he offered to cut the onions. 'God I'm starting to weep,' he moaned. 'Have you got any sunglasses?'

'Yes, why?'

'To stop the fumes getting in.' And he put them on and continued peeling. It was too funny - this beautiful man wearing sunglasses at seven pm while he cut onions.

Dave wandered in and ate the last of the spaghetti. 'Delicious,' he munched, offering to roll a couple of joints if someone made him a coffee. They smoked and drank coffee on the verandah listening to a record by J.J. Cale. 'It'll be a full moon in a couple of nights,' Dave said.

And without thinking Jane looked across at the onion peeler. He was looking back at her, smiling strangely. 'Weird wild things happen on full moons,' he said. She looked away almost embarrassed, as if there was some secret between them.

The days unravelled. She could see the moon growing full, spreading its golden orbs further into the sea of darkness. There was a strange ease in the house, a certain warmth of unseen things. 'It's that friend of yours,' Dave said one night, 'he gives off good feelings, this rat hole's getting a new face;' going off before Jane had time to plug him further.

At night she lay in bed watching the moon high above the clouds, wishing she was by the sea with some nice man to hold her and say nothing, to feel the moon's strange eerie warmth enter their bodies, some unseen electric force silently sweep through them.

The next night as she was leaving to go up to her room, he held her hand lightly for a moment looking into her face. 'Goodnight,' was all he said.

And she positively ran up the stairs. What was going on? For an instant she felt hot as a coal, mmn lady, watch it. She thought of him lying there in his beatup sleeping bag with feathers streaming out of the sides. She could sense something was wrong. Perhaps he and Sharon were breaking up. But no that was ridiculous, they wouldn't give up now, they were planning to live in the country, get away from it all, get some peace. They'd both written to her talking of 'their future'.

Friday night he had tea already cooking when she came home from work. Martin and Dave were hovering in the kitchen like cannibals. 'The food'll be ready in half an hour or so, I hope you like rice.'

'I do, I'm amazed. I'll go and have a bath while it's cooking.'

And she lay soaking in the hot water, smiling at how considerate he was. She dried herself thoughtfully and poured a liberal amount of cologne over her body. Very carefully she painted on some pearly mauve eyeshadow and put on a purple kaftan.

'Mmn, you do look good,' he murmured, as she drifted into the kitchen.

Dinner served, Dave mumbled, 'This offsider here of yours isn't a bad cook,' hoeing into the last of the oysters and cheese crackers.

'I think he's pretty good myself,' Jane laughed.

And Martin decided to celebrate the cooking venture with a few good pipes of hash. They smoked and laughed and Jane told them about the negroid toads in full living colour detail. They played records and smoked and talked and smoked and lay on the floor and smoked and drank coffee and smoked.

'God a drink'd go down well now,' he said, turning to Jane who was propped on one elbow on the floor.

'I think I'm incapable of moving.'

'Of course you're not,' putting his arms round her waist and dragging her to her feet. 'We'll go and have a few beers then come back here eh?' And it all seemed so intimate and warm as they wandered off down the street. 'Look it's a full moon.'

'I know,' he said, silently taking her arm.


A couple of beers turned into a couple of dozen, everyone was raging out of their minds, racing off to parties, chasing women who'd only be chased when they were drunk, breaking glasses - an ordinary night. 'It's like a madhouse up here,' he shouted, 'It's been a long time since I went drinking like this.'

'Well you should do it more often.'

'Sharon never drinks,' he muttered. 'Two drinks and she's absolutely smashed.'

And she remembered Sharon always holding herself in, playing it gentle and safe, quite the opposite to him. The usual setup. There always had to be a stabiliser, usually the woman.

But she was in no mood to moon over someone else's problems.

Who gives a shit. By half past ten they were back at the house dancing round to the Stones. Martin had dragged Cheryl along, and even Dave had a woman wedged in a corner, absolutely raving at her. Joan and Harry were staggering round drunk as usual, and that nut Alistair had turned up wearing his habitual runners and singlet, the famous bicycle rider. He had hornrimmed glasses as if they grew out of his face, and liked to spout Joyce though usually he never said a word. It was almost a party.

'I can't go on,' Jane was laughing, 'I feel too smashed, that was really good hash.'

'Well let's look at the moon then,' dragging her upstairs to the little verandah off Dave's room. The night was cool and bright, sweet air drifted across their cheeks, the moon turned a silver face down towards them.

'You look beautiful,' he said suddenly.

Something in her drew back, 'It's only the light.'

"Purple's the colour for sorrow. Are you sad Jane?'

If only you knew, she thought, there's too much to tell you. She was thinking how beautiful he was looking under the moon, how easy to be with, not screaming and pulling at her, demanding justifications.

'I'm feeling rather tired actually.'

'Shall we go to bed?' he asked suddenly.

And she looked down at her hands resting on the balcony, vague, stoned, empty, unable to answer.

'I'd like that very much,' he said, taking one of her hands and holding it to his face.

And she could think of absolutely no reason why they shouldn't, whether it mattered or not, she was stoned enough to feel almost indifferent, but heard herself lamely say, 'Do you think we ought to?'

'Yes,' was all he said.

The bedroom was filled with a soft moon glow as he pulled back the covers and helped her undress. It wasn't till he kissed her she felt something snap. His tongue was inside her mouth like a darting lizard. Yes, she thought, yes, the desire took her like a canoe swirling down a river, a tumbling throbbing avalanche sailing blindly without a course. She murmured vague mad things to him and he replied touch for touch.

They lay back flushed, smiling, staring at each other. Incredible. 'Jane, I feel crazy,' he said, kissing her, 'I've always wanted to do this, have you?'

'Yes, yes,' she heard herself reply without even thinking.

There was something like shock covering them as they lay there smoking cigarettes. 'It's just the full moon,' she felt weird enough to laugh.

'It's just the full moon,' he echoed in the darkness. 'I feel wonderful, don't you?' as if for reassurance.

She hadn't felt this good in ages. Perhaps it was only the combination of the meal, the hash, the booze, the full moon. Liar, she said to herself, it wasn't of course 'just that.'

Next morning they stared at each other in silence, 'Well hello,' one of them said, and they both smiled crazily.

He got up and looked out the window, 'It's a beautiful day, want to get up yet?'

'Okay,' and he came over and kissed her.

Somehow they floated through the day; lay around in the sun in the backyard, went to the shop, made pots of tea, played records, talked. A whole Saturday drifted by. Dave came out proudly from his room with the woman he'd been raving to the night before, made her breakfast/lunch and hustled her off to the pub. By nightfall they were alone in the house and feeling hungry.

'Let's go and eat eh? Or would you rather stay here?' He seemed incredibly considerate or maybe he'd always been like this and she just hadn't noticed, after years of being 'friends.'

'We could go to the Chinese, I feel like something mild,' and she went upstairs to change.

There was dinner and king prawns and much fussing over a bottle of mead to have with the meal. They smoked French cigars and smiled like cheshire cats. They strolled back to the house and carried cups of coffee and biscuits up to the bedroom. They lay in bed holding hands and watching the moon. 'It's as good as I always thought it would be,' he said to her, and that made her shiver way down inside, like a small cold fear, a deep secret being unlocked.

And she deliberately blotted out any thoughts of Sharon, but wondered if he was doing the same. She never doubted his sincerity - they'd known each other too long for that. 'I feel wonderful,' she whispered, lying back on the pillows.

Sunday they went to the movies and saw *Willard,* the movie with the star rat in it. They laughed themselves stupid, clutched each other in mock terror, and Jane insisted he buy her a Crumble Bar. For an instant he thought of Sharon - funny they should both like Crumble Bars - but the irony flashed by. Fuck it! It was too early for guilt. He felt in general a fine sense of release.

They made love that night like crocodiles on a rampage, and again in the morning before she went to work.

'What's got you? You seem rather pleased with yourself?' Dot asked Jane as she was standing by the coffee machine gazing into space.

'Mmn, oh nothing, nothing at all.'

Dot glared at her, unable to prise her open.


That evening getting off the bus, Jane couldn't help walking that little bit faster, pretending she wasn't of course. Christ, anyone would think she'd never had a man before.

He was talking to Martin and Cheryl in the kitchen and had made a casserole for dinner. During the meal it was hard to keep from touching him, brushing hands and eyes. After they'd eaten he went off to the pub alone, and she took a long hot shower, was already in bed reading when he came in slightly drunk.

'The moon's on the wane,' he mumbled. She nodded.

'You know do you? you know,' looking at her strangely. 'There seems to be more moon up here. It must be my head,' tapping his forehead.

'Perhaps you can see the sky more up here,' Jane said stupidly. 'Yeah, wider horizons,' he muttered.

And she felt that chill realising he was twisting her words, they were coming out loaded, ready to burst. Into what? Damn it! Rockets of the heart. Bleeding flowers of lost years. She lit a cigarette, wishing there was something tangible to hit at, wishing this quivering and straining and awkwardness would stop. Like digging in a mine and discovering strains of gold, hints that there is more, then finding no common use for it, no way to convert it, make it workable for every day use. Was that it? Bleeding rationalisations.

He didn't make love to her that night, and lay there with his back turned. She went off to sleep dreaming of spiders enmeshed in dark sticky webs. In the morning he kissed her vaguely then went back to sleep.

Tramping round the restaurant she thought, damn it you fool, he's going back to Melbourne, and what about Sharon? For the first time she stopped to think of her. Sharon had been one of her best friends for years, though they didn't see that much of each other. Some friend eh? How would she ever be able to visit them now? Gained a lover, lost a friend? She realised that what -had happened had been inevitable. She'd never dared admit it to herself before, but it had always been there. It must have been for him too. Perhaps that's what he'd come up to Sydney for? No, it was something they'd just stumbled on at this time. What time? The right time, the right time. Bleeding circumstances that's all.

She refused to think about it anymore. He must be feeling pretty confused himself and it was he who had to face the real music - she was getting out of it lightly. Getting out of it? They'd hardly got into it.

The rest of the day passed in a boring stream of coffees and ten cent tips from stingy businessmen who leered over their menus. He wasn't there when she got home that night, only Dave who called, 'Well what's going on Janey? Where's your lover friend?'

She lit a cigarette and looked acidly at him, 'I don't know where he is, and he's not my lover friend.'

'Well you seem to be having a pretty good time the pair of you.

Come on Janey, I think it's wonderful really. I haven't seen you looking so happy in ages ... but he's married isn't he?' Yes Dave, yes.

'Never mind,' trying the ridiculous approach. 'It'll work itself out,' patting her on the shoulder.

'That's the trouble, there's nothing to work out,' hurling his hand away. Bloody Dave, used to having three women a year, burying himself in his veterinary studies - he seemed to have the notion that people could be handled as simply as animals. Lame dogs. Sad cats. Ugh these! cliches.

She. went down to the pub later and found him there slumped over a beer. 'How'ya doing?'

'Okay,' he mumbled. 'Like a drink, what can I get you?'

She felt as if shewas intruding. 'Sure you don't want to be alone?'

'Come off it jane, you know where I want to be ... or do you?' giving her one of those strange looks.

They had a few maudlin drinks and she kept hoping he'd cheer up.

But he didn't, and they didn't. There was an awful sadness between them as they stood in the doorway looking out at the thin moon.

'Let's go for a walk eh?' he said suddenly, pulling her arm and slopping beer on the floor.

'Okay, okay,' she felt angry with him and very confused.

They wandered through the streets in silence, a few feet away from each other. The moon hung down, a skinny fingernail without a hand.

'I wish I could be in Persia,' she said, kicking at a stone, hearing it rattle down the empty street.

'Persia doesn't exist.'

'Oh allright!' she burst out suddenly, 'Just quit it! Are we going to walk around all night feeling sorry for ourselves? I thought you were here to have a good time? Well let's have it!' and she started off down the street away from him. Damn it! If she was honest she'd be in bed with him right now. But would he want that?

'Jane?' she heard him calling behind her.

'I want to fuck you, stupid!' she called back crazily, 'I don't care what happens next!'

'Jane you're insane,' he yelled, catching up with her.

'That rhymes,' she said nastily.

'Aw come on, take it easy, let's have a good time then.' And they hugged each other fiercely.

They went home and did just that. Fucked each other stupid.

'I think I might even love you,' he murmured.

'Me too,' she heard herself reply.

It was wonderful and terrifying. It was delicious and bitter. They wanted to go on interminably in that crazy state, sniffing each other, biting, entwining their bodies like snakes.

At seven thirty am. the alarm went off and Jane realised she had to go to work. Groan, groan.

'I'll make some coffee before you go,' getting up and putting her Chinese dressing gown on, it came to his thighs.

'God you're lovely! You're inscrutable!'

'Madame Butterfly at your service,' bowing from the waist.

It just went on and on. She got on the bus like a normal human being feeling completely abnormal, found a seat, bought a ticket, smiled at the conductor, looked at the aliens groomed and strained into place, felt smug as shit, had dialogues with herself like 'you filthy swine,' smirked revoltingly out of windows, smiled like Narcissus at reflections in passing shops. She was even on time for work, they almost dropped dead. And whistled while serving coffees. Dot was positively seething with curiosity.

What do they do with themselves? Jane was thinking going home on the bus - do they secretly masturbate in the wardrobe, screw their wives silly to erase the corporation from their minds, fight and hurl the six pm. dinner at their wives? What the fuck did *they* do?

You're a bloody vulgarian, she chuckled to herself getting off the bus.

They spent the next few days fucking like siamese twins, knitted together, forbidden cradles - how he seemed to glow and extend now she'd discovered his body, how much more easily he could be conjured up, after all these years of 'friendship.'

Friday night he unexpectedly turned up as she was finishing work. 'Let's go to dinner,' he smiled, 'it's my choice this time.' He took her to a Hungarian restaurant where they drank wine and ate schnitzels, talked about jobs, not working, places to live.

'You've seen the place where we're living in Melbourne,' he was saying, 'It's just too small for two people, you start driving each other crazy after a while.'

And she was nodding, being objective, hadn't she wondered about that very thing?

'That's why Sharon and I are moving to the country, we've been thinking about it for ages. You know what Sharon's like, can't cope with the city really .. .'

'Yes it'll be good for you both, you should have done it years ago .. .'

'Yes maybe we should have,' he was looking away from her, 'Maybe we should have ... '

And she just couldn't talk any more, was staring into her glass, the half empty vessel shining under the candlelight. She was terrified by his duality, his capacity to have both of them, to have been a bridge for her to walk over gliding into happiness, bringing her laughter and offerings, of resurrection, of incompletion. Why did she have to cling to his gifts, to want the strains of gold to claim her? He would go back to his wife taking their secret to her - he would transplant the mirage.

And she felt cold and rejected, almost bitter towards him, almost doubting the moments they'd shared. As if she hadn't known. The inevitableness of their futures. This attraction to dream.

# Reality Fragments

All this reality, these bits, you have to find a way of addressing yourself to the mirror, a way of getting it together and blowing it apart, then catching the pieces if you can. They just want my body, he said to her as he was taking her. They just want to get at me, taking both breasts in his teeth. I'm tired of giving them my sperm. He's dancing in a hallway of long black swords, he's a gargantuan lover who ends up drained of love.

The last time I saw her she'd shaved her head and joined the Divine Light. The way a junkie can get to be high with friends. Just imagine it, she said, it used to cost me money, now I just turn on for free twenty-four hours a day. It's a new kind of junk, I told her. God you're cynical, she replied.

All these bits, these bits. He's written a story about it, that X was lesbian and Y came over to shoot up Mandrax in the bathroom. He wasn't there but his girlfriend rang him to say, come over and get me out of this, I don't know what's happening. Lock yourself in the kitchen, it's your scene, he said, then went back to sleep. He wrote the story the next day.

Will we work all this out? She got a note that read, I love you, but he rang his wife while still in her bed. Do you have to be so indiscreet? she said. Gee baby, you're being unreasonable, why don't you be realistic? Do you have to be so insecure? So she mentally burned his wife and buried her in a coffin resembling the shape of his penis.

The reality was merely a way of talking. The book of poems she'd written was better than watching TV. It took up more time. It's just a matter of getting the stuff together, of blowing it out and catching the pieces in your hand. Reality, the fragments, and the meat the sword cuts.

# Dark Roses

He had rather dark olive skin, a shiny face framed by black hair as pungent as seaweed, a kind of ironic twist to his mouth, the lips drawn over very white sharp teeth. He was Spanish and came from Barcelona or someplace where people danced with bulls, and he still wore the scars of horns on his back. He had a beautiful body, yet covered in tiny scars like embossing on a Persian carpet - tiny roses of knotted skin where intrusions had been made. It wasn't as if he was a violent man, but he had this attraction to explosions. Call it passion if you like. He could be very gentle and tender in his body of wounds.

I really love women.
I cannot express myself, my English is very bad.
Why do people say I am a bastard?
Nobody's interested in my mind.
Why do poofters always want me?
People here have no soul.

He glittered in his dark skin and flashed the whites of his eyes. Being a drunkard brightened the sparks, it also deepened the scars. It made it very difficult to talk with him, through a haze of alcohol that blackened and charred his sight, that made his skin burn as if he lived permanently on the Equator. Where do you look when someone is crawling round your floor barking like a dog, or falling against walls, shattering his mind; you can see the pieces fly?

Coming from another culture. made him aggressive to his adopted home, and being called a 'wog' didn't exactly ease anything. It was even worse to talk with his own people - the sort he would never mix with at home. So the pub was a marvellous mirage, a palace of possibilities and desires. He could be anonymous and a star simultaneously, merging with the drinkers in a burble of broken English, drawing things to him - men, women, drinks, in a flow of uninterrupted sparks. Perhaps he was addicted to the friction, that was why he burned so freely? Strangers came to him for his blaze, yet turned away when the heat transferred to them. He could attract and repel in one flash of his white teeth. What was the purpose of his fire? Everyone knew he was igniting himself, the days rolled on a sea of pyres.

I know people hate me. It's because I get drunk.

I hate being drunk, I know I am stronger than the drink. When I hold a bottle in my hand I know I can beat it, the demon in that bottle.

Then why have the bottle at all? Because I am stronger than it. Then you're just testing yourself?

No, it's just this bloody country. I drink to keep my heart warm. The demon keeps you warm?

No, the demon gives me nothing. That's why I am stronger than it - I like to give things to people.

Then it's just a game you're playing.

No, the demon's playing it on me. She's been with me all my life.

How can the heat be bearable? The doctors say he has an ulcer. The psychiatrists say he is schizophrenic. His mother says he's her beloved son, his father says he is not a man. His lovers say he is magnificent in bed. His landlady says he's a good and quiet tenant. His boyfriend says he's the only good man in the country. His women say he is a bastard. It is also said he's a madman, a thief, a poofter, a bum, a mummy's boy, a dago bastard, an alcoholic, a potential suicide, and a Latin rat.

And what do the roses say? The little whorls of skin encased in the flesh, so smooth under the finger, almost blossoming under the lips? He rolls on to his back like a beautiful greasy seal on a bed of empty bottles. He's very quiet when he's sober, his eyes floating off into black pools of silence, the lips not moving - mute. Nobody can force an answer from him - why does he dance with hot coals?

He's full of hate for this country, yet when he tries to go home the demon pulls him back. His parents want him to marry and live in a whitewashed villa with a black haired woman and many children. They thought he would be a success in this country, yet his letters tell them he's an unknown foreign labourer. Like a black alien beetle, he moves across the streets waving different antennae encased in strange armour. He passes through jobs, drugs, men, bottles, women, fights, hospitals and friendships like a creature possessed, burning everything in his landscape, finding the pavements inevitable in their smack against his skin, the glass a kind of mirror when they extract it from his body.

The dialogues are always confused. I don't remember what I did. Somebody just punched me and I had blood all over my body. I had it running from my head. They had to give me some kind of injection.

He just came on to me - this poofter, ran his hands all over my body, and started kissing and hugging me and saying I am beautiful. I didn't want it but what could I do? I couldn't say go away you bastard. I couldn't say that. I don't want to be like that.

He made love to me and it was horrible. He put cum all over my trousers and dug his fingernails into my back. I have the marks still on my body.

I don't remember much. But I'm not a poofter. They just never leave me alone. They think I am handsome. It's not like this in my country.

The women here are like wood. They lie there with their legs open. I put myself inside them and try to make them have an orgasm. But they never do. Women in my country bite and scratch me. The women here have beautiful bodies but I cannot talk to them. They are bourgeois and only want me because I am different. They get upset if I muck up their clothes. They tell me I am destructive. They just want to tuck me.

I'm not violent, I don't like fighting. I take Valium to calm my nerves. It is the alcohol I suppose. But I am stronger than the demon.

People here think I am a fool. But I am stronger than them. I walk down the street with my head up and my back straight. I see them bent over, whining like dogs.

If you talk to a madman you find it hard to know what is fact or fiction. You always wonder if he's a mirror for your wildest desires. You always wonder if you're a voyeur and merely getting cheap thrills. There's nothing cheap about people suffering.

When will he return to the country of his people? He says he is frightened to go back, knowing what his parents expect of him. Others tell him it's not a country which matters, that you should be able to live anywhere. That he must find some home in himself. He says there are many homes buried in people's flesh, when he is deep inside them. He says it's the only time to feel beautiful - when the heart is lying on the sheets, the body burning like the Equator.

# Letter of Complaint

Rain, rain. The dead heads bullnecked roar: The dead eyes spit, uncertainty of tattered pools. Rain, rain. Lagoons are seething about to burst, crocodiles sink teeth beneath the surface, glint of scales. No armour is worth its weight unless it stings. The mouth unfurling fire, the teeth knowing what to rip, the lips knowing what to kiss. Smack, smack. Of false affections. As eyes break into red-veined maps, journeys of the world, of eyes sick with seeing, eyes spewing crumpled visions.

They try to tell you to lick their shoes, from the ankle up, subserve, they try to force you, screws of repression, twisting you in, tight, to humiliation, breaking your back, only then allowing you to speak. Hear, hear. The crows in line, teach you to peck before you can walk, teach you to break before you can fly. The compromise, the fucking compromise, eating your words, your self respect. Armies to kill the heart. The dead heads roar. The slave man's chains.

# The Time Device and Christmas

*The Visitors*

He walks drunk into the house, it's Xmas day at one pm. and he's wearing a singlet with a slogan reading: 'This garment is made of pure shit.' The ex has brought his friend Roberto with him who's also drunk and wearing a blood-stained Pelaco shirt not in the way they're advertised on TV. They collapse into one of those grain-filled sack chairs which immediately oozes across the floor and crushes a pot plant in the fireplace.

'Hi doll, I thought I'd wish you a merry Xmas.' He empties a bottle of Pilsener and tosses it across the room. 'Got any booze?'

'I've got a bottle of Royal Gold whisky,' she feels obliged to say, 'I didn't expect to see you here.'

'Well thanks a lot babe, I'll just borrow some of that whisky while you explain why you didn't expect to see me here.' Paranoia arrives. 'Oh Christ!' she says, turning away (they've been split up for six months), 'I'll get some glasses.'

'It's really good to see you,' he burbles, gazing at her like a sad porpoise lost in the big bad seas. 'I've been doing a lot of drinking you know.'

'I know,' she says, refusing to feel guilty. And she hands him the Royal Gold and two glasses and stumps off to the opposite end of the room.

He's wearing that forlorn naive mask of his, that heart-pulling sentimentality she just can't stand; that 'look what you've done to me babe' expression, 'but I'm still here being nice to you. Because I love you' business. He is in fact sitting on sticks of dynamite, with fuse wire, gelignite and detonator all ready. She of course is the time device, the trigger.

'Can't say I thought much of the company I saw you in the other week babe,' he was tossing up, clanking Royal Gold into glasses and. hurling one in Roberto's vague direction. 'I really was surprised to see you running round with that sort of rubbish.'

Jesus! 'I don't think it's any of your business,' she manages sweetly. 'Anyway I don't think much of your efforts, wasn't that the Bulldozer

I saw you with the other night?' (The Bulldozer is a well-known lady of illicit demeanour and habit, weighing about 13 stone.)

He ignores that. A cheap lie eh?

'I just can't understand it, love (bringing in the intimate 'I understand you so well' tone), after what happened between us I thought you'd be a little more discriminating, that's all.'

As if he can talk. You've got to be desperate to go to the Bulldozer. 'I don't wish to discuss your opinions of the company I keep!' and she swept out of the room, furious that he'd come round. Oh she was sick of being a time device, of the fuse wire in their words, of the dynamite under the Xmas tree. And they say it's merry, this time of the year.

### The Dinner Table

'Christ, it's a small chicken you've got,' Roberto is saying, tearing one wing off, 'Got any more whisky?'

Around the table are Peter, Joan, herself, Ali, Roberto, Ex and Boris is under the table.

'I can't stand garlic,' Ex is saying, as Ali plonks a garlic-covered salad on the table.

'It keeps the vampires away,' Ali growls.

'These wogs are all the same,' (Ali is Spanish), Ex mutters to her, not quite loud enough for Ali to hear.

The chicken has been torn apart, pity there's only two legs and two wings. Bottles of herbs, chocolates, nuts, octopus legs and olives are strewn across the table.

'Would you like a sucker?' Ex shouts, tossing the remains of an octopus leg near Ali.

Three bottles of beer fall over as Ali suddenly leaves the room. 'The salad's beautiful,' Joan whispers.

'I think it's got too much garlic in it,' Peter snarls. They kick each other under the table.

'Why don't you just give me a joint?' Joan whines.

'Here, make yourself one,' Peter tosses a half ounce of grass on the table.

'*Ooh,* how lovely,' Roberto moans, promptly rolling himself two. 'I notice you haven't got any dope yourself,' Ex says to her.

'I don't really worry about it these days,' she answers.

'But you sure enjoy smoking other people's,' Ex laughs, giving her a vampire's smile. 'We never could agree on ideas of considerate behaviour.'

'No, we never could,' she agrees, watching him drink the last of the Royal Gold.

'I hate Xmas!' bursts out Peter (grass has a habit of making him expressive), 'It's so much' bullshit!' sucking on his fifth joint.

Ali has returned. 'In my country we have true Christmas, we party all Christmas eve into the morning, so on Christmas day we are resting and relaxing.'

'You're just wiped out, that's all,' snorts Ex, 'You Christmas with mamma and poppa, don't you?'

'So what is wrong with that?' bristles Ali.

Boris the dog chunders under the table, he has eaten too many octopus legs.

'What a horrible smell,' comments Joan.

'Just because it's Christmas,' bellows Ex, gallantly staggering to the kitchen. He returns with a wettex and half a cup of detergent which he hurls under the table. 'Now to get back to us babe, when are we going out?'

### The Aftermath

Ali is lying drunk in the sack grain chair singing a Spanish folk song out of tune. The TV is on with the sound turned down, and the radio is playing. Joan and Peter have had a fight and Joan has gone to her mother's for the night. Peter is upstairs smoking his 90th joint for the day. Roberto is huddled in one corner reading aloud from *Flowers of Evil* jittering as the D.T.'s come upon him (been an alcoholic for ten years). 'I just love these poems,' he intones, as his left leg breaks into a spasm across the floor. Ex has gone off to acquire some more booze, saying he can't bear to see her consorting with rubbish like Ali, and will punch him if he gets the chance. She is sitting on the floor smoking her sixth joint and drinking a glass of *sake*. It's been a heavy day, Christmas is always heavy. She recalls that Simon and Marcia dropped round and at one point Ali was talking about his country and Simon had said, 'Gee, that's really mongolian, man,' and she hadn't known whether her hearing had gone mad, whether Simon was mad, or whether it was really quite an ordinary comment to make. Maybe she was off the air because it was Christmas Day. But she'd decided there was something very strange about the conversations she'd heard that day, but when it came to writing them down she couldn't remember them properly. It was the intonations that were so important. Like detonators. Without that little silver detonator all that fuse wire and gelignite and timing and dynamite wouldn't go off. She decided that most dialogues were sounding insane lately, without conclusion or reason.

She sat there listening to 'You're So Vain' on the radio and wondering how a song like that could get on the Top 40. She made some more decisions: she didn't want to see Ex at all, Ali was very boring when he was drunk, she would not try to rehabilitate Roberto, she would stop Boris from eating exotic foods; that Christmas was bullshit - all those rituals of getting as smashed as one can. To rejoice? in the new-born King. She didn't approve of kings. And she remembered that porno movie she'd seen where Santa had come down the chimney and screwed this big-boobed girl in a stocking. And everyone had laughed. And how every Christmas she thought about what she'd done last Christmas, and how next year, next year she was going to be having a respectable relationship, and not be drinking, smoking dope and trying to remember rude lines of dialogue; and thinking things like gee everything's changed so much since last year she could no longer tell where the dynamite lay (it seemed to be all around her), and what form it was in, and who would light the fuse (was it self-igniting?), and was she the detonator or merely the time device? It was very confusing and would be next year and the year after, and what did she expect not being monogamous and under 21 with all those tinsel dreams in front of her? She decided she'd keep a book for writing lines of dialogue in as they happened, that this would entail becoming a voyeur instead of a time device, a kind of rationale for the perpetuation of these years.

# The Pantomime

In the beginning was the word and the word was ... light of a thousand stars and eyes, arms, lips, the tongue in words, words, babble of sound and a thousand dancers.

The couple were in fancy dress. The woman wore a Spanish dress of emerald green, and he wore skins, suedes and a camel hair hat that'd done much travelling. They both wore masks and were drunk. I breezed past and nodded hello, they laughed and the woman threw back her head revealing a tattoo on her throat. The man arrogantly held out a bottle of Tequila and I swigged on the flame drink. Wonderful. The woman smiled at her lover and I felt I was intruding, so I moved away. Later ...

It was another one of those Revolutionary Bullshit New Left Anarchist Affairs, meant to be a dance, with four rock 'n roll bands and a lousy PA system which screamed whenever it was approached. I hadn't worn fancy dress though most people had, but I felt okay in velvet dungarees and riding boots.

There were many painted and sparkled faces. One was black and white striped to resemble a zebra, another was so pale with chalk, his eyes and lips blackened like bruised blood he seemed to be a zombie, a Dracula, a half-risen anaemic apparition of death. He swung his jewelled arse in a mime of women. I felt bored by these pantomimes. The whole dance seemed to be full of gays. Everywhere I turned men were flashing at each other, men gazing in mirrors, I could not tear Narcissus from the glass - I felt like a slimy charmer offering out-of-date wares.

'Oh Carol, don't let it steal your heart away/I've got to learn to dance if it takes me all night and day' ... the band was thumping out some good rock 'n roll and more like: 'I hear you knocking but you can't come in! I hear you knocking but ...' with a bopping Crash Craddock type singer, and a few lights splattered about the stage. So Charlie cruised by and dragged me onto the floor to  dance among his gold locks and glittered fingernails. Sweat poured off his gilded face and Charlie was transfixed by the motion of his hips ... I saw the couple again.

They were dancing very close against each other, the woman swaying her many layered skirt was biting into the man's neck. She had a long red scarf tied around her head and trailing down her back. With eyebrows arched above her mask she suddenly untied the scarf and pulled it carefully through her fingers. The man was staring at her, a strange, almost pained expression on his face - like dying people have, a delirium of ecstasy and resignation, having suffered so long yet knowing they're going to die. She was pulling that scarf slowly through her hands, slowly as a cheetah, swaying and sliding her hips, her red lips drawn back over white intense teeth.

It was a dance of deliverance, of ritual. It was an old and sad story ... in the beginning was love ...

The Spanish lady held the scarf across the palms of her hands, then tied it through a buttonhole in the man's shirt. Then smiling strangely she tied three knots in the scarf and let it fall. It hung down past his knees and he stared out through his mask. Then she moved back and began stamping her feet. The man tossed back his head, his face half in shadow, threw up his arms and danced as a lord. He caressed the scarf and blew on it as if it was one of his feathers...

Charlie was wriggling and flashing at a transvestite to one side of him. I'd no idea what I was doing, my attention was on the couple. They were gliding in, out and around each other, their masks glinting, their expressions frozen into capture, caught up by the story. Yet why did I feel sad as I watched their celebration? Wasn't this the oldest story in the universe without which there'd be no light, no force, no life? Was I fearing their inevitable separation? Fearing their completeness, their privateness? Had I said inevitable? Couldn't I picture them in thirty years time, their expressions now beautiful, their masks fallen aside, their faces full like fruit?

I remember my mother telling me true marriage wasn't possible; 'You have to compromise,' she'd said. 'That's where the lie begins. They won't let you be yourself, these men, as men aren't themselves. But as a woman you'll be expected to bear more. If you develop a real difference they'll reject you. So you'll compromise inevitably, unless you choose to live alone. It probably started with Adam and Eve - that woman came from man's side and drew him into temptation. I don't believe that story, but we are a part of man, the other side he's frightened to face. Perhaps we're the shadow which leads again into light, and here the two join. But this's sheer idealism! All my three husbands have tried to mould me, change me and crush me. I can tell you about marriage - it's compromise.'

Ouch! So this was the legacy I'd been left, as I danced with a queen who seemed to know neither the man or woman in himself; as I danced watching a couple ensnared in a lovers' net, and me doubting their capacity to love.

'Oh darling, isn't she gorgeous?' Charlie was positively drooling in my ear about the transvestite who seemed to be almost on top of us.

'Oh yes, lovely,' I murmured, feeling sick to death of these charades, it's more acceptable to be twisted these days. Anything but normal, sane, heterosexual, moral; anything but healthy, unaddicted, consistent, constructive. We have this preoccupation with neurosis, morbidity, suffering and darkness. I found myself dancing stupidly not wanting to compete with the transvestite. After all, Charlie was here to get some action. I waved to the transvestite to come forward in her cheap satin shoes. At least get on with it! Charlie was squealing as I moved away feeling the temperature soar to 140.

You're a bitter twisted woman I told myself, feeling threatened by all these queers. Nothing moralistic, just an inbuilt sense of injustice - like first they keep us in chains for 40,000 years and now they tell us to go to it, while they turn to admire each other. Hopefully we'll turn to our own sex and discover our clitorises have been given back to us.

The Peacock Male has returned ... but why does he dress and gesture like a woman? He carries that head of platinum-streaked blow-dried hair for himself and the admiration of other males. Has he ever asked a woman what her image of him is? Probably, and she's just as twisted. She's got no tits, no hips, shorn hair and a face of make-up. She's belted, jeaned, booted and T-shirted. She can openly say, 'Fuck me baby ... now,' and see how little difference there is between us. We can all share the same deodorant ... if I threaten you as a woman then I'll dress more like a man. If I'm tired of this male role then I can gesture like a woman. Interesting ... we change sides ... and become invisible.

I'm sick of this confusing bullshit and the fact that ninety percent of the men here appear to be gay. The women drift in and out between them like beautiful lifeless decoys. It's a pantomime of the most monstrous fears. It's a pantomime of highly painted decadence, a delightful show of death. Nobody will make a pass at me and I'm too square to make one first. I don't feel desirable if I ask a man to want me. I'm ensnared in pantomime and conditioning, Mum you didn't tell me your husbands were homosexuals.

The couple are laughing again. The cowboy has the woman's hand in his mouth and is circling her like a wolf. She's laughing and following in delirious consent. I know they're both drunk but they look as if some inner fire has consumed them. I stand near them staring as the band breaks into 'Shake, baby shake'. The Spanish lady hands me a drink, they're on their third bottle of Tequila. I toss back some flame water as they motion for me to join them.

We're dancing now, the three of us, weaving in and out, a couple, a visitor, a recipient - the woman is thrusting her hips at me. The man seems remote behind his mask, his lips aren't moving. The Spanish lady laughs and curls her arms at me, beckoning in a peculiar ritualistic way. I feel her mocking me ... 'Shake, baby shake,' my eyes travel down to her ankles veiled in black stockings. She's mysterious, joyful, and I desire her though I can't see her eyes. She stamps her feet and stares straight through her mask at me. I don't really want to taste her flesh, but I'm drawn into her ambience, their ambience, these masked lovers. I'd simply like to lie with them, peacefully, and absorb some of their happiness - not lust for them in pursuit of some erotic pyramid.

I believe they could be the sleepers within the pyramid, and climbing their flesh would not take me to them.

The cowboy watches me closely and draws near in careful feminine steps. He turns in a flair of swivelling hips and rotates his arms above his head. He draws me into him like a drunk yet I know I can't quench him.

He's playing with me because she's watching. He's flirting with me like a woman - he's matching her for her maleness with me. I shy away, ridiculous, and they move towards each other. I see sparks fly from them as I fall back into shadow.

So Charlie is enfolded in the transvestite's dress, mooning softly to the music. I dance with a man in a Mao cap and red armband. He has a mock cardboard machine gun strapped into his belt. He has shoulder length hair and delicate hands and wrists. He couldn't fight his way out of a paper bag. And I feel terribly masculine in my velvet dungarees and wrinkled riding boots. The flame drink has almost put hairs on my chest. We dance on in a charade of emptiness. Sometimes I'd like a moustache.

Around one a.m., I staggered from the dance after my revolutionary finally vomited on the floor, and I hadn't offered to take him home. The night outside was deep and cold black, the moon hanging in a half quarter, the gold bright as an Indian morning.

'In the beginning was the word, and the word was … ' why did I have this damn line running through my head? I walked along and saw the lovers, arms around each other, swaying along the pavement: Suddenly the Spanish lady broke away and ran to a huge canvas mask that'd been hung from the balcony for the pantomime. She disappeared behind it with only her black legs showing beneath it. It flapped in the night air. A laugh rang out. The cowboy threw up his hands, 'Do you think I can't see you, lady behind the mask? You must be the woman of veils. Mmn. I think I must capture you.' And he darted behind the mask and I could hear them hugging and buckling out of sight, the woman shrieking with delight. 'I love you,' I heard them whisper as I dodged past.

Perhaps they'll dream of me and I'll remember their gestures. Not the sham sexiness of David Cassidy or the androgyny of David Bowie, the false beauty of Gary Glitter, the plastic surgery of Marilyn Monroe . . . I'll probably never learn to walk down a staircase like Marlene Dietrich, to ignite men's hearts, to approve of a husband's lovers. I want to remember the privateness of that couple, the love and power in their dance … I'd like to think they haven't compromised, that my mother will be proved a liar. That Adam and Eve remain in the Garden of Eden. Sheer idealism? Don't tell me.

# The Silk Trousers

There was something in the way the sun slashed its long violent arms through buildings and balustrades, the way it crawled along the streets wrapping itself round peoples' legs; the way it suddenly grabbed them full on the face, the whiteness of their eyes becoming brilliant as steel. There was something totally naked and savage about the sun in this place, it ripped through clothes and skin, it showed no remorse, no softness or subtlety.

The monkey man walked round the corner, his grimy red lungi hanging loose about his legs. The neck of his white kulter was showing a frill of perspiration, his face was powdered in fine black dust. He walked slowly like a panther, his flat cracked feet padding silently down the lane. He had wound the monkeys' leads around his hands and shoulders; he smiled a long hungry red-toothed smile.

The Australian girl was sitting by a tea stand drinking a glass of thick sweet chi. She heard the monkey man rattling his drum, saw the wooden ends of the strings cursing and flaying the skin. She saw his fine-boned ankles, the toes like dark barnacles clutching the ground, then the two monkeys: Mr. GoGo and Mrs. ComeCome. The monkey man smiled at her with his red teeth and long red tongue.

'Dance, madam? You see dance? Monkeys dance very good.' But she was looking away feeling suddenly hot, embarrassed, slurping her tea, shaking her head. That man's smile and those black sloe eyes were too ... obvious, too ... intense. She finished her tea and turned hurriedly down the lane, the drumming rose and fell behind her.

There was something in the way you could walk every day and meet the same characters, the same red-eyed jumble of hot-faced players, the same steaming breaths, the familiar resigned eyelids. And with the sun doing its best to treat bodies like Cellophane, and the streets covered in sweating garbage, and white cows perspiring by water pumps - it was a strain, a permanent fantastic movie, a furnace of actions where everything was possible, everything available. It seemed as if there was no reality other than this one, that tomorrow was as impossible to conceive of as yesterday - that the only reality was the seething present, the here and now.

Helen was a tourist in the streets of Calcutta. Whenever she rounded a corner in that labyrinth of dark bodies, she seemed to find the monkey man beating his drum in the furious sun. Some of the hustlers who hung around the tourist quarter told her he was a fake; 'Fake man, fake, monkeys don't dance,' so she never stopped to see. 'Him want rupees, too many rupees,' they'd hiss at her. So she'd go past listening to the drum, catching a glimpse of Mr. GoGo baring his teeth and stamping his legs, and Mrs. ComeCome doing backflips and getting tangled in the leads, as she could never keep up.

Days melted by, the sun was too hot and she felt hysterical in the heat, seeing her trousers stick to her legs, her T-shirt cling to her neck in a coat of sweat. The world was stark and blinding and searing, mornings exploding on the streets, trees standing absolutely erect under the blaze. Not a wind or cloud. And the monkey man materialising out of stone walls, with grinning teeth and drumming hands, his hair and body like tongues of fire. He was too dark, too hypnotic, with his teeth scarlet from chewing betel-nut and his eyes of fathomless black. To be white and blonde and deranged from the sun ... it's only this heat, Helen'd rationalise, making me crazy, that man's Svengali, he seems to know who I am, to read what I'm thinking, to have something on me.

Yet day after day the sun would penetrate her hotel room, would not stay out in the courtyard, hung around on rooftops, exhausted fans which spun lazily round and around flicking dust onto the sheets. Even the beggars moved back on the pavements to find a little shade, sat cross-legged with pieces of tin or cardboard or rag over their heads. Children bathed naked at the water pumps, cows stood patiently flicking their tails as they were doused with cans of water, and rickshaw-wallahs lay listless under the shade of their rickshaws, smoking chillums or sleeping or tossing stones in the dust.

The monkey man padded about lathered in sweat, absolutely serene.

He always carried a long thick stick which he used to beat the ground with in time to his drum. Sometimes he waved it like a wand to clear people out of the way, or as a marker to show the monkeys where to sit, or where to fight. He twirled it like it was gold. It was imposing, magnetising, a conjuring wand which made him powerful and distinct from all the others.

'Hello madam, hello.' Helen was sitting at a tea stand trying to cool down. 'What a fine day today.' He was smiling and bowing from the waist. He had knotted a piece of red rag around his neck to match his lungi. 'See monkeys dance, madam, see monkeys dance,' the wand hovered near her leg.

She shook her head, 'I don't want to see the monkeys dance. They don't dance, do they?'

'Oh yes madam, dancing. But we smoke chillum? Too hot for dancing.' And Mrs. ComeCome did a backflip then lay down puffing. Mr. GoGo was staring at her, grimacing. Helen finished her tea and began walking away. The monkey man wound the leads around his shoulder and sprang after her.

'We smoke chillum eh? You smoke ganja? Come madam, inside, quite safe, on corner. We smoke chillum eh, keep cool. Come now madam, come.'

And this had been going on forever - him scattering his monkeys in her path, getting Mr. GoGo to clap his hands every time she appeared, getting Mrs. ComeCome to curtsey and backflip every time she saw her. Insisting. Insisting. The sun beat down in giant leaden bars. She was perspiring heavily, and the thought of a chillum was intriguing. They reached the corner and he strode up a dusty staircase calling, 'Come madam, come, no harm. Please sit here, you cool down.' And he was spreading a piece of newspaper on a step, in view of the street, and out of the sun. She went up and sat down.

Two Indians were asleep further up on the landing, and the stairs went on and up into the grimy building that had no end. The monkeys threw themselves puffing on the stairs, and the monkey man was smiling and muttering to himself. Could he be smirking? Helen was uncomfortable sitting on the newspaper in her $40 silk trousers, her very clean Biba T-shirt and Chinese velvet sandals. Yet she'd come thousands of miles to be here, to do ... just this. She wanted to be sitting in rags, to have her hair in a plait, smudged kohl round her eyes, a jewel in her nose, gold bangles on her wrists. But she sat there very white, very Western, and very conscious of her seeming affluence.

There was something in the way the monkey man was so close and hot and steaming, his dark pores glistening, his eyes so curved and black. She felt she'd been sitting here on this staircase for thousands of years, sitting with this monkey man and the monkeys in the dust. Sitting and being and not thinking, the heat melting her thoughts, the sun giving power, being consumed in fire.

And what could they talk about? The monkey man knew little English, but enough to hustle a rupee from her to get some ganja. He whistled down the staircase and a small boy appeared, he gave him the coin and the boy disappeared through the shimmering doorway. It was as if he stepped into another dimension - the heat was insane, a rearranging of matter seemed very possible. He might return in the shape of a fish.

One of the sleeping men woke up, spat on the landing then curled up like a cat and went back to sleep. 'Where is your country?' The monkey man was leaning towards her touching her knee. She saw his long black nails slither across the silk trousers. She felt hot, absolutely burning, the staircase was an inferno filled with brown dust. She smiled. The boy came back with some ganja rolled in a piece of dirty newspaper. The monkey man produced a chillum from under the folds of his lungi and began rubbing the ganja. He spat into his palms, rubbed and rolled, rubbed and rolled, smiling and smiling with his patchy red teeth, his eyes running over her like coals leaving burning trails behind them.

'I'm from Australia,' she answered. And suddenly she could picture the monkey man over there, somewhere in the bush with his oily black hair glistening in the sun, padding through gum trees, washing in creeks, stopping to pick a banana or knock a pawpaw from a tree with his stick. She could see him in the desert squatting by a fire, gazing into the darkness, listening into the never-never. She could see him over there as dearly as she could see herself here, sitting on this staircase in the dirt with the monkeys - a long time ago.

She had nothing to say to this man, words were unnecessary; she had no poem to deliver him, no prayer from a white God - the moment was complete, nothing more perfect than to be in the present. A few million years lay between them. Any concept of black skin and white skin seemed ludicrous at this moment. They were melted puppets on a burning stage. Shiva was Buddha and Jesus and Allah as he watched over their gunja smoking. 'Bom bo lay, bom bo lay,' a great flame shot from the chillum ~ she was out of her mind and into the present. They were midgets in a mighty circus, a cosmic circus of infinity, out of time, out of history, into one gaping eternal moment.

Yet the thought of this Indian touching her was absolutely terrifying. The thought of lying with this man underneath his dirty lungi, of touching his pocked cheeks and running her tongue over his scarlet teeth, of spreading her fingers through that oily rope hair was ... too much, too much to keep her in sanity. She had no room for escape. She was in a maelstrom of desire with no intelligible moral code to rationalise her feelings towards him. The reason she felt love for him was the reason she was terrified to touch him.

There was something in the way the staircase swayed and swayed, the monkey man's lips swayed, the girl's head swayed in confusion. She was sitting in her silk trousers like a Maharani in a cheap novel. Perhaps she was consorting with demons, this man was almost master over her heart. But then this man had experience with the heart - this way, the way of existence here. It was Calcutta not Canberra, that honeycomb of barren souls.

Suddenly a South Indian appeared and swaggered up the stairs. He stopped at sight of them, a nasty smirk covered his face, he began babbling in Hindi, taunting and goading the monkey man. The tirade went on - this filthy beggar man and this wealthy white lady - the monkey man was smouldering, he moved his stick dangerously near the man's legs. The South Indian grabbed the end of it when suddenly Mr. GoGo flew at the man's hand, biting out a piece of it, the blood flowing bright and fast. Then he leapt back hissing, spitting and baring his teeth. The South Indian howled and sucked his bleeding hand.

'Scum man, scum,' the monkey man was screaming. The Indian was wailing and cursing. Mr. GoGo was springing about hissing and letting out strange shrieks. Mrs. ComeCome ran back and forth with knitted brows, tangled in her leads and spitting furiously. What a commotion! The two sleeping men on the landing woke up and began jabbering hysterically. The whole staircase was throbbing with sound. The monkey man lashed the air with his stick, while Mr. GoGo tried to bite one of the men's shins. They all screamed and thundered down the staircase into the street. Silence. The shimmering doorway was empty. Clouds of dust hung in the air. Helen sat dreaming on the newspaper as if it was a magic carpet, perspiration clinging to her hair.

After hundreds of years the monkey man returned and threw himself at Helen's feet. The monkeys flopped on the stairs, puffing and obviously hysterical, their eyes still out on stalks. 'Scum man make trouble, I protect you, be here,' and he patted his heart and smiled like a demon. Now he was muttering of secret meetings, planning other chillums in dark corners, 'No trouble madam, not seen.' And he meant he'd take her where no one would find them. He was touching her silk knee, he was leaning so close. She was stifled and exhausted. He wanted to possess her.

She was not dressed in a sari, with gold bangles and henna-dipped feet. She was absolutely white and Western, and though she'd escaped time she couldn't escape into his flesh - he might stick gold pins through her breasts, bite the hairs from her yoni, cover his lingam with spikes to twist into her, chew her ears till they ran blood - call up monsters from other karmas to give him power to possess her.

She would run before he devoured her. That man retained a power from thousands of years of spiritual birthright - he had tiger and elephant Gods to advise him, and she had culturally nothing. A twisted image of a son of God impaled on a wooden cross, a pale corpse who made her a sinner before she was even born. Two thousand years of guilt to absolve - no time for dancing or feasting or love-making. Her heritage was ashes, penance, and self absolution through repression. Was this her only power? Was there no other God to help her? Had she been torn from a man's side and let out of Eden to suffer the guilt of creation? It was predestined - this hideous lot of suffering. She was powerless, there was no time for love. She must assuage a few thousand years for being white, for being civilized, for committing the original sin. she would be punished for wanting to love.

The monkey man was towering near her. He seemed to be surrounded by a faint blue/white light. He wanted her for all the reasons she wanted to escape herself. It was ghastly! What twisted fate! Suddenly she leapt up and ran down the stairs through the one-dimensional doorway, down the baking street of lava. It was hell and orange madness. She thought she heard drumming rising and falling behind her. She didn't stop.

Seven nights later Helen stepped from a rickshaw near her hotel. A black gleaming shape rose from the shadowy wall. It was the monkey man swathed in red. The monkeys' teeth flashed unnaturally white. She thought she heard a hiss. The monkey man held something out to her, he opened his hand and she gasped. It was a beautiful stone chillum in the shape of a man's genitals. Each hair and curve and blood vessel was perfectly chiselled. It glistened smoothly in his black hand. She saw a flash of inhumanly bright eyes as she ran to her hotel room.

Then a low down sound of drumming. The rhythm continued all night under her window, throbbing and throbbing into the black air.

She heard bells drift far off across the city, the rumble of rickshaw wheels bumping along streets of dust. Faint sounds of singing. Black crows squawking over garbage. White cows bellowing in the darkness. The chattering and shrieking of monkeys. And always that throbbing, that drumming rising and falling in waves, ancient, timeless and terrifying. Next morning she took a plane to London.

# *End Dialogue*

You are afraid ..

No, the world is too ugly.

There are easy ways out.

As a woman you must give birth. Children are what we build on.

Then I wouldn't be with the man I love. Children make love material. They are the third thing which binds and separates.

But as a woman it is your duty. To give to the world.

Which world?

But it's basic, he said, leaving his last fuck.

The lovers are leaving. We are trying to dance with all our extremities.

# *The Incomplete Portrait*

I am not making love at the time of writing this story, in fact it's been some time since I felt any sunlight streaming through the skin. But then, you don't want to read about me making love with anyone other than yourself, you don't want to know that I came to you wearing a string of loves, adorned and possessed ... It's more important for you to spread these artefacts between us, to have the story that is the distortion, the guidelines of another structure between, us - us the watchers, the voyeurs, the discontent, the incomplete - to construct our ropes and hangings on the page, to cosset ourselves in images, cocoons of love made readable - the 'literary' story - when our private acts fail.

I write this because I do not trust this 'distance,' this portrait that does not resemble the original matter, this abstraction that allows minds to swing between acts and bodies. This personal mythologising to make others love us, when we may be unlovable with our six o'clock shadows and bad morning breaths. I've had enough of this distance, this literature of myth, as I sit here encased in skin linings, watching my wrists and fingers move across the page propelling thoughts towards you.

You will not admit to the body of the matter, undress the meat of the story, unravel the carcass to see if it's still breathing. You will not confess to the mirror that your ego does not approve of. I am expected to appear virginal, undiscovered, mysterious, veiled. I have to project an image of wholeness, yet not based on anything actual - on the gulfs of love I may have fallen into, the drunken horsemen burying spurs in darkness. You want me to come to you pure as a lake you may see your own reflection in, blue enough for you to realise the lake has depths, yet safe enough for you to never ride to the bottom of. I should tell you your love is like no other - when what do we use as criteria if not our comparisons? As a woman I must lie, I must propagate your self-made image even if I don't agree with it, even if it is false.

Tammy Wynette is whining on the jukebox: 'Stand by your man' as I sit in the lounge having been refused admission to the public bar. And I think about the time of loving, the moments frozen into poems and stories, inaccessible, unrepeatable, over. My body drapes itself on a chair - this loved, hated, sometimes infected, resurrected body; this receptacle of sadness and semen, of blood, celebration, distortion. And I sit knowing I can't keep writing stories of unsuccessful love affairs, of husbands gone back to wives, of lovers in terror of commitment, with the hungry reading these lines as a source for recrimination. I should be constructing myths to keep my image intact.

My resume could read:

I must not undress heroin pushers.

Reveal that (a) has small genitals.

(y) is obsessed by his mother.

(q) was being unfaithful (as I was probably his mistress).

(m) beat his wife up.

(p) has been giving infections to women in that crowd for years.

Though (r) wrote a story proving it's the women who always carry infections.

That (t) aborted his girlfriend and is secretly homosexual.


It's no good exposing these foibles only to become classified as a man-hater, a castrater, a neurotic terrified child. Somehow the artefact must propel gently from the tip of my breasts, never quite revealing its true form, skilfully divulging snippets of flesh and cheek without unveiling the active ingredients. (Like a negligee, people say a woman is more desirable this way than nude.) Somehow the woman must write from a peculiar 'other' set of sensibilities, grinding her tenses and mincing her participles; she must convey her sense to the idiosyncrasies of a 'masculine' logic, and measure up to its structures and laws.

To be a good male writer might be to have 'guts'; to be a good female writer might be to have 'cunt' - yet somehow this predetermines exposures which are not acceptable, and possibly self-righteous.

You do not want to read about my sitting in the VD clinic waiting to have my vagina scraped. A neon sign is flashing: 'There is no stigma attached to having VD but you must come in for a check-up, you could be spreading this disease.' You do not want to know about it because it's unpleasant, unfeminine, ugly, unromantic, unnecessary… yet you'll read Burroughs' description of gouging holes in his thighs with a safety-pin to try and find a vein. You'll read that and say there's some point to it - he's a junkie who may influence others from taking drugs, possibly having some positive effect on the society - because his experience is so vividly ugly. Yet a woman writing of an instrument stuck up her cunt is being 'self-indulgent' as the doctors make notes. And you won't read of the girl who was gang raped, preferring to refer to statistics and 'she probably asked for it didn't she?' You will think these stories unnecessary, indicative of a female mind gone sour.

Reading the dust jacket of his serious novel concerning the 'sexual badlands' the heroine:

(i) Gets beaten up and assaulted by his long time 'literary' buddy.

(ii) In chapter 3 is pregnant, hooked on speed, and kidnapped by a gang of poets.

(iii) Chapter 9 she has her first lesbian experience because she can no longer have orgasms with a man.

(iv) Final chapter she's a 'used up bag' and burnt at the stake at a ritual literary dinner party.

The female fiction writer will be dealing in areas of bitterness; she'll be making phone calls to her sexuality to see how she's all wired up She'll be desired (if pretty), admired, abused, mythologised, attacked.

She will be symbolic of Marilyn Monroe (can you walk down a staircase that well?), Kali, Janis Joplin, Medusa, Isadora Duncan, Lilith and blah blah. She will never be being 'objective' enough and of course will be a fascist.

The criteria:

Sublimating - because she has no children.

Unattractive - because she is intellectual.

Neurotic - because she's competing in male territory.

Dangerous - to other women because she's not a housewife.

She will also be a ballbuster, a bitch, a slut, a predator, etc. She will be more fiction than her words on paper, and worth more if she's tragic (see previously listed symbols). In her case the actions will be read more than the words. The story will be the looking glass and the dress she wears, her perfume and her capacity as a lover.

The rejection:

Kate Millett has noted that D.H. Lawrence was a fascist and a woman-hater - he thought women with short hair were masculine, and his heroine rode away only to be sacrificed as a spike of sun loomed towards her, undoubtedly the symbolic prick. It's already gone down that Lawrence's ethic is invalid because he was reportedly impotent. Yet didn't he spend a lifetime struggling with his woman in an attempt to understand her? Maybe he didn't succeed, but wasn't he railing against sexual strictures for both men and women?

It becomes increasingly difficult to talk in general terms. The fiction is insurmountable as fiction is always paradoxical. And this piece of writing is one-sided and hasn't reached definite conclusions. It is not even a story.

I am trying to look at the artefact, whether it be sublimation or extension. The shores of your body are littered with truths. The page should fuck back - I can't think of a more reasonable premise.

Lightning Source UK Ltd.
Milton Keynes UK
UKHW011527141022
410475UK00002B/170

9 781922 698476